Dulci's Legacy

Other Books by this Author

Memory's Hostage

Praise for Memory's Hostage:

"Memory's Hostage will delight lovers of historical fiction and mystery." -Chad Novacek, Amazon

"A compellingly written novel" -Gail C., Amazon

"Tight, well-researched, and well-plotted" - Shanna, Amazon

"If you like Wilkie Collins' Armadale and The Woman in White, you would love this one." -Larry H, Amazon

Dulci's Legacy

Margaret Pinard

TASTE LIFE TWICE PUBLISHING

Dulci's Legacy

Margaret Pinard

Cover Design: Melody Simmons, Ebook Indie Covers

Pubished in the United States by Taste Life Twice Publishing

ISBN-13: 978-0-9898506-3-6

Printed by CreateSpace, a DBA of On-Demand Publishing, LLC

*To learning to trust your own vision,
something I learned with my parents*

Chapter 1

*   *   *

God, I hope this place is better than junior high, Dulci Oyselle thought as she passed through the tall double doors into Glace Cove High School. It was the first day of the new school year, the air was crisp with chill, and Dulci yearned for something *different*.

She'd grown up in Glace Cove, and it was so small that her eighth grade class had consisted of thirteen individuals, twelve of whom she'd known since birth. The one 'new' person was Carly Smith, whose family were still considered newcomers after ten years in town.

Despite the smallness of the pool however, Dulci had few people she considered friends. She was small for her age, and rather timid. She was not athletic, in a town which chiefly valued their hockey team and deep-sea fishing prospects. She had one friend, her best friend: Mehron Tebnek, who was the daughter of her father's friend, Tuotu Tebnek. Don Oyselle and Tuotu worked together on the scientific research ships that left from Cape Breton Island, often on long sea voyages bound for the Arctic Circle.

They'd hung out a lot this summer, talking about what would make high school so much better than junior high, while their dads were out to sea. Mehron dreamed about the freedom to go out on dates when she got her driving license in a couple years, but Dulci longed more for a larger circle of friends. No offense to Mehron, of course, but she wasn't musical, and Dulci loved music, especially the Celtic music so celebrated on the Island. She'd been learning to play her bodhràn, and secretly hoped to find others interested in folk music at the high school, so that she wouldn't only be playing with septuagenarians. And while Mehron had already been asked on a couple of dates, no one had yet asked Dulci. She didn't think it was likely that high school would be any different on that account. With mousy brown hair instead of her friend's shiny black, and skinny awkward limbs instead of well-developed running muscles, she thought it better to concentrate on her music and her studies. Her parents supported the academic focus, praising her awards and honors.

The materials she'd gotten in the mail said that school would start with an assembly in the large gymnasium, where students would sort themselves into homerooms and advisory groups, both new concepts to Dulci. She flowed along with the human traffic to the gym, rubbing shoulders with the elbows of what had to be a senior basketball player on her right. She looked up briefly, caught the surprised glance of blue eyes under curly hair and a ball cap, then looked forward again, lest she be swept away by the undertow.

As they filed into the gym, she glanced around, remembering the shiny sealed-wood flooring and the white-painted brick walls from when she'd cheered on Mehron in a Junior League basketball tournament last year. Her eyes scanned the bleachers for her friend, but there was no sign of her, so she reluctantly climbed up to the higher rows to sit. The principal was standing patiently at a microphone at half court as the rest of the student body settled in: all told, about 120 students.

When Mehron finally did enter, it would have caused

a scene for her to reach Dulci, so she caught her attention and shrugged, indicating they'd find each other afterward. The principal, Mr. Bracethwaite, had the typical welcomes and bluster to get through, which elicited cheers from the non-freshman classes, and polite applause from the faculty, who were ranged on folding chairs to his left and right.

Finally he got to the useful information. Pointing to his left and right to temporary tables set up behind the faculty, he said, "Now, you'll all have lots more information to process, but we'll be accomplishing that in your homerooms, and then in your advisory sessions. We'll be calling out names now by class for those assignments. And since they do deserve some privileges after three years of," he paused here for a wink, "*very* hard work, let's call the Seniors first!"

Cheers erupted from the right side of the bleachers, where most of the seniors had sat together. It seemed a pretty small group to Dulci, and in fact when they'd all clambered down the aluminum benches, she'd counted only twenty-nine students. *Smaller than the other classes then*, she thought. *Maybe not everyone makes it that far.* They filed out the far exit doors to their homeroom classrooms.

Next came the Juniors, sitting in the middle seats, and higher up. Thirty-nine teenagers rose up around her, although the last student to walk down when his name was called was sitting just a couple rows below her on the left, so not with the rest of the class. *Is he new?* Dulci wondered. That didn't happen often, and would have undoubtedly been remarked upon by Mehron before now if she'd known about it. *Probably just a loner, or a huge nerd,* she thought, but changed her mind as he turned to the principal.

Mr. Bracethwaite was shaking the hand of the tall kid with whom she'd rubbed elbows in the sea of humanity outside. He added for the benefit of the high school students still sitting in the bleachers, "Finn MacDonald is newly moved to Glace Cove with his family, and I'm sure we'll all do our best to welcome him here to our school, eh?" Finn was obviously nonplussed by this extra attention, but rolled his shoulders back and smiled slightly at the principal. He ducked his head and slid a quick glance over to where Dulci was sitting, but didn't seem to meet anyone's gaze, before quickly turning and heading for his assigned table and paperwork.

Dulci felt her heart rate pick up a bit, just learning who he was. Why was that? It wasn't like he'd be interested in her. Maybe she'd get to meet him if Mehron wanted to talk to him though. The thought ignited a little fire in the pit of her stomach, and she was suddenly impatient to get her assignment and tell Mehron about her close encounter.

* * *

The fact that Mehron had athletics first in order to practice with her basketball team meant that they had almost no classes together, even as freshmen. Before lunch period, Dulci finally spotted Mehron in her science class, and joined her at the high table set up for lab experiments.

"I totally have something to tell you," Dulci whispered to her while the teacher was writing something up on the white board.

"Ditto!" came Mehron's reply, accompanied by a mischievous grin. "Is it about the new boy?"

"What?! How did you—" but Ms. Simmonds turned around and she had to bite off her reply.

This teacher asked questions all period, and watched the students like a hawk, so it wasn't until lunch that the girls were finally able to continue their conversation.

"You first," said Mehron.

"You probably have something much juicier to report. I was just going to say that I bumped into him on the way to the gym. We had one of those, you know, *looks*." That may be exaggerating it a tad, but what the heck, she thought.

"Oooooh! Well, that's a good beginning. I have more background on him: his family's originally from here, but his parents went out west to earn money in the city, in Calgary, I mean, and they're only now coming back because they lost it all in the last recession. So they're opening up the old house outside Baddeck and they're going to try their online business here."

"Wow, that's rough luck," said Dulci. "I wonder what he's into…"

"Well, Karen Nelson says that he mentioned being to see a lot of Shakespeare plays, and Andrea Padron says that he seemed pretty good in algebra, but Noreen Patel says his schedule hasn't been decided yet because he's going to try out for the hockey team…"

"What? How have you gotten to hear all that stuff already, when we've been in class all day?"

Mehron smirked. "I was in the toilet when a big flock of sophomores came in to gossip at break. Just keep your ears open, Dulci." She winked. "Anyway, the *Provocation*'s set to come home tomorrow, so ya wanna meet up at Slip Two an hour before? I'll probably have more dirt on the new boy by then…"

"Dirt! Mehron, come on. Give him a chance to be normal, even if he is a newcomer. And my mom's bringing me down early before she goes shopping in town, so yeah, I'll see you there."

Chapter 2

* * *

Slip Two was not its usual quiet self the next morning. Instead of gulls swooping and waves lapping, the soundtrack was loud and man-made: cars and boats, all preparing for the big ship the *Provocation* to arrive and disgorge its contents. Dulci sat in the middle of a pile of neon green rope on Slip Two, where one had the best view of Slip Three, the widest and most modern berth available in Glace Cove's small wharf. She watched the gulls float seemingly without effort, tried to block out the diesel chug of the boat engines, and only wrinkled her nose occasionally at the smell that could only be trash washed up with the tide and baking in the sun.

Once, she knew, Glace Cove had been a fair-sized industrial port, with ocean perch fishermen leaving for the long arctic summer, trappers collecting lobster closer in, and the bigger ships coming and going with their cod and mackerel for processing. That's why the town had stayed clustered near the shoreline and between the fingers of seawater creeping in among the island's hills. But the recent recession had changed all that. It was why two of the three fish processing plants had closed and were now being sold off to developers for vacation homes. The people would have to earn money some other way.

Their friends the Tebneks did better than most in their community of Mi'kmaq Indians, but they by no means owned a vacation home. Tuotu had worked hard and stayed at a low salary position at a medical lab thirty miles away in order to provide for his family. When Don Oyselle had lost his specimen collector to a better-paying job down in the States, he'd found Tuotu's application for the job the most compelling, and their partnership had become a firm friendship in the intervening years. Now that their daughters were fast friends as well, Tuotu sometimes lectured Mehron on what a good example Dulci was: serious, studious, and respectful of her elders. Occasionally he reminded Mehron of this while Dulci was there, which always made her feel awkward. Mehron was all those things already, Dulci knew, she just didn't care about the grades the way that Dulci did. She had basketball to put her heart into.

But for now, no lectures. Dulci could see Mehron clomping across the old wooden boards as she alighted from an old blue El Camino. The long toothy-looking car added its rumble of diesel to the din as it roared away. Dulci saw her friend's clouded face.

"What's wrong?" Dulci asked as soon as she was within earshot.

"Just Jesse. He's threatening to leave again."

"Oh," said Dulci. This was another subject that made her feel awkward. The Tebneks, she knew, had problems with their son Jesse, but she also knew Mehron didn't like talking about the details, just complained about having an older teenage brother who was out of his mind. Dulci didn't know how literally to take that characterization, especially since he had actually threatened to hurt himself.

"Is it school?" she asked.

"Could be. Who knows? He doesn't really need a trigger, although he was doing pretty well over the summer, not having to be near other people at the farm."

The farm was a plant nursery further inland set up for

disabled adults and troubled kids to work in. They pounded dirt and shoveled fertilizer in order to make money selling the plants, fruits, and vegetables at the annual sale.

Mehron sighed. "My parents haven't signed the papers to force him to take the meds, but this time when Dad gets home, I think he might." She turned to look Dulci in the eye. "This time he threatened me, too."

Dulci couldn't imagine the Jesse she remembered from five years ago ever threatening his kid sister, but her heart went out to Mehron, to be in such a hard place. "Mehron," she said softly, touching her sleeve.

"I know, crazy, right? He joked it off immediately, but for that one second, he looked so angry he could have hit me. We just don't know what else we can do, you know? We've tried all the mental health services, all the tribal council free counseling sessions, even the sweat lodge! They still haven't gotten rid of the hallucinations he says he has. Nothing has."

Dulci kept her hand on Mehron's sleeve. "Don't worry. Something will work. He'll get better."

A whistle blew nearby, and out of the afternoon fog, the outline of a ship started to take shape. Voices called out to one another in the husky island accent, crew greeting harbor folk after months at sea. Just in time, Dulci's mother Olive joined them. She tucked her pressed trouser cuffs around her heels so they wouldn't get dirty on the dock and leaned her willowy form against one of the cleaner wooden columns. Another sound blew, an octave lower: the foghorn.

Activity blossomed as the ship came in. It took a half-hour for it to dock, lay its plank down, and start spilling out its crew and precious cargo. Many of them greeted Dulci and Mehron as they passed by their slip.

"How long'a you been 'ere, eh?"

"Aren't your feet little blocks o' ice themselves, I'd like to know!"

"Mornin', ma'am. Hey-o, girls. A good trip, that. Ask

your pop to tell ye all about it, now."

Tuotu and Don were the last to emerge from the hold. Don stopped to give Olive a quick kiss and claimed Dulci in a brief hug before stepping back into the line of traffic to unload the samples as quickly as possible. His broad shoulders in the fur-lined parka were visible amid all the bustle, and Dulci followed his movements, barely containing her excitement, and relief, at his return.

Several more trips from ship to government shed near the dock, and they were satisfied. Tuotu locked up the last padlock and handed the key to Don. They both turned to the trio on the docks and shouted out their traditional return greeting for the girls, "Happy New Year!" They all laughed and Dulci's family piled into the Oyselle station wagon to head home, cares forgotten while in happy company.

Chapter 3

* * *

The excitement of the Homecoming of the Dads, as Mehron described it, lasted the whole weekend. Each family tucked into its own homecoming supper. Dulci imagined Tuotu and Joan talking over the news about Jesse, and hoped they could find some solution that would keep Mehron safe but help Jesse. As an only child, she didn't know what it would feel like for your brother to be a ticking time bomb, but she figured it wasn't great.

Don and Olive spent the whole weekend together with Dulci, as they always did when he first got home. Olive's legal clients, who usually called at all hours of the night and expected her to drive around all hours of the day, knew her strict limits at this time of year. Dulci liked seeing how close her parents still were, especially when compared with the many other parents who had divorced. She thought they lived a sort of charmed life, especially since they hadn't been hurt in the last recession, as so many others had. She was lucky to have the parents and the home that she did, she knew. The two-story well-built home, the screened-in-and-heated porch, the week-long summer camps, these were luxuries that most other people in town couldn't afford. At 13, Dulci had already noticed the differences this created between her and some of the other kids whose parents worked on the wharf or in the quarry. Her hope was that in the bigger pool of Glace Cove High, the differences wouldn't be so noticeable, and she wouldn't be treated like the 'little rich girl.'

While she only had one class with Mehron, she hoped to make friends in the other classes. Also, she had noticed amid the announcements in her school newsletter that there was a call for extracurricular activity ideas. On Monday, she put in her request for a music club, dropping her paper in the suggestion box outside the school office. There was no telling how long it would take to get started, but she cautiously got her hopes up.

Wednesday it was time for Advisory again, after which she navigated History and English Literature, and now she finally had the break to see whether any extracurricular announcements had been posted on the bulletin board outside the school office. She was heading there with her backpack over one shoulder, her gaze on the ground, thinking about what it would sound like to be drumming along with pipes and fiddles, when she stopped short at a pair of large white sneakers in her path.

She looked up.

It was Finn MacDonald.

He was smiling uncertainly, but definitely looking at her and waiting for her to speak.

"Finn MacDonald, right?" she asked, knowing it wasn't the best opening line.

"Yeah, I think everyone now knows who I am, but I don't know anybody yet," he said. His words joked, but his eyes, Dulci saw, looked earnest, almost pleading.

"Well, my name's Dulci Oyselle," she said, brushing a stray piece of hair behind her ear. "I'm new here too actually," she said, having found a joke of her own.

"Really? I thought I was the only one."

"Well, I'm a freshman, so I'm new to this school."

"Ahhh, I see. Funny." Finn grinned, and a little of the seriousness fell away. "Listen," he said, glancing down to the floor, "I've been wanting to find you since we bumped into each other last week. Maybe we could go out sometime?" He looked up again at last, gauging her reaction.

Dulci was floored. It was the *second day of school*. This was their *first conversation*. She was a *freshman*, for god's sake.

"Umm, yeah. I think that'd be cool." Immediately she kicked herself for sounding so *un*cool. "I mean, I'd like that." She couldn't let on that she had to check if going on a date was okay with her parents; she *couldn't*. "Is it okay if I let you know later? I mean, when were you thinking?" She was getting more flustered, and could feel the blood creeping up her throat, suffusing her cheeks.

"Oh, I hadn't really thought about it, but maybe this weekend? I'm trying out for hockey this week, so I guess I'll be at practice every evening," he said, his expression turning sheepish. His blue eyes stayed on hers, not flicking to her reddening skin. *Thank God.*

"Oh, right. Okay, well, I'll let you know tomorrow then, OK?" She was losing the power to breathe normally, and feeling the sweat start to form at her temples. She gave him her best pained smile, then hurried away to the toilets, where she promptly locked herself in a stall, covered the seat in toilet paper, and sat on the edge.

The blood was pounding in her ears and she made herself breathe long breaths through her nose, out her mouth, just like the exercises she'd seen people do for First Aid. After five or six of these, she felt a little calmer, and tried to remember what she'd been about to do. The music club! Maybe there was still enough time in the break to—but just then the bell sounded, and the fifteen-minute reprieve from class was over.

Her next class was French, which she mostly tuned out of, since her dad had spoken French with her at home since she was a toddler. They'd probably end up promoting her out of this basics class. Maybe then she could take an art or music elective. Her thoughts slipped back to the encounter with Finn. It seemed so…strange. Not just that she'd never been asked out on a date before, and not just that he hadn't known her before asking, but the way he seemed so needy, like he was asking her out because he was being pushed to do it. She really hoped it wasn't a joke or a dare.

After French, it was math. Dulci's previous test results had placed her in Geometry, which was mostly sophomores. More people she didn't know. But she tried to pay better attention here, since she worked hard on math at home to get ahead. It was something her parents expected of her, and she didn't want to disappoint them. This lesson wasn't particularly hard though, and while they were silently working out the classwork problems on the white board, a messenger knocked on the door and came in with a note. Mrs. Graham took it and looked up. "Dulci?" she called. Dulci raised her hand. Mrs. Graham walked down her aisle with the note and laid it on her desk, then continued looking over students' work, giving comments here and there.

Mrs. Graham may not have been curious, but all the students around her sure were. Three or four glanced in her direction, their eyes dropping to the note. What could it be? Dulci felt suddenly seized with fear of some dire accident at home.

> **Delightful suggestion for a Celtic Music Club!**
>
> **As music teacher, I'd be happy to organize some practice sessions and a performance if we're up to it.**
>
> **Please stop by Room 212 after school today to discuss.**
> **-Mr. McKenna**

Oof! That's all it was. Dulci breathed a sigh of relief. She smiled a little to herself as she went back to solving the Pythagorean theorem problems, and managed to ignore the stares of the sophomores with complete equanimity.

* * *

Several more subjects passed by in a whirl, Dulci's mind returning more consistently to her encounter with Finn than to the teachers' words. At last the final bell rang. She hurried to the locker rooms to change out of her P.E. uniform, and got her things from the gym locker. *Room 212. Mr. McKenna.* She wondered if any other students would be there.

She entered the open door marked 212, and saw an older man in the far corner at a desk. She didn't remember him from the assembly last Friday, but maybe all the elective teachers hadn't been there?

"Mr. McKenna?" she asked. He looked up.

"Ah, and you would be Miss Oyselle?" He motioned her over to his side of the classroom.

"Well, yes, only it's Wa-Zelle, not Oy-zelle."

"Ah, French, of course, forgive me." He smiled and she could see him better. He was perhaps in his late fifties, with patchy red and white skin, and longish graying hair. He wore a gray suit and a white shirt, more formal than most of the other faculty. His accent had traces of British in it, but more than that Dulci couldn't place. She shrugged in response to his apology and waited for him to continue.

"Yes, so, a music club. Your suggestion particularly mentioned Celtic music. Do you have a specific interest in that tradition then?"

"Yes. I play the bodhràn. I've been practicing for two years, ever since I saw a performer at the Celtic Colours festival. But I mainly use YouTube videos and instruction videos, and I've only played with others a couple times. I think it would be fun, though," she finished.

"Of course! Music is therapeutic for oneself, but its real expression can only be found with a group, and an audience. At least that is my opinion," he said, smiling broadly again. "So you don't know of any others in your class or on the Island who might also be interested?"

"No. I thought you might know of any here at Glace Cove High?"

"True, and I do." He gave her a wink. "So first thing tomorrow I'll slip in an announcement to be read during Homeroom for any students to come to a meeting on Friday. How's that? That should give me some time to get some music parts together and find the spare instruments."

"Um, sure, that should be fine," Dulci stammered, wondering if it would conflict with her plans with Finn. Oh well, that wasn't even certain yet. "Yes, that sounds good. Thanks, Mr. McKenna."

"My pleasure, dear. And since I've got a bodhràn handy here," at which point he got up from his desk and reached to a shelf above and behind him to pull out the wide shallow drum, "would you like to give it a test run? That way I can hear you, and then maybe I'll jump in." He handed her the drum, which had a tipper hidden in the hollow back, while he pulled out a violin case from under his desk.

Dulci picked up the tipper and held it loosely like a pen, flicking her wrist experimentally. She picked up the drum from its crossed timbers in the back with her left hand and tapped a few times in the center to hear what it would sound like. Her drum at home was slightly smaller, so she would start softer with this one. She traced the pattern of her favorite song in her head, and waited for the muscle memory in her right hand to take hold as she tapped.

It did at the same moment Mr. McKenna started in on his violin, picking out an instrumental tune she recognized. She faltered a moment as she looked up, taken out of her own reverie, but then took up the beat again. *Keep the beat but hear the others.* Soon she was pounding the tipper sharply and switching time to a more insistently militaristic march. She smiled as she heard Mr. McKenna's sliding bow switch along with her to a sharper, lower sound. *And what if there were bagpipes*, she wondered.

Just as she was going to alter her pattern to a less powerful one, she felt a blast of wind in her face that made her eyes water. She blinked away the tears, using the hand with the tipper to wipe her eyes. When she could see again, the question to Mr. McKenna about the sudden gust died on her lips as she looked around to see she was no longer in the classroom, and the music teacher was nowhere to be seen. She felt rooted where she sat, and all around her was a dark, cold, eerie mist.

Dulci turned toward the door she had come in, and saw only the crest of a snowy hill, lit by unobscured moonlight. She turned back to the wall where the windows had been, and saw a wavy sort of light, like she was looking through that old bottle-glass vase of her mother's. She looked up. A bright three-quarter moon and several stars visible. *Am I going crazy?* A muffled sound came from the direction of the hill, and she had an overwhelming fear of what she would see top the rise. It wouldn't be Mr. McKenna.

The sound became louder and more human, the sound of someone shouting through a pillow. Her eyes fixed on the rise, Dulci saw a large shadow outlined in the mist. The figure stumbled, and Dulci saw two hands shoot out toward the snow. All she could see were the large masculine hands, glowing pale in the moonlight. The rest of him was covered up in layers of clothing, maybe wool. The man grasped at piles of snow, and Dulci saw why. When the dry powdery snow dropped back to the earth, it stuck in clumps, a dark muddled red color. He was cleaning blood from his hands.

After a few turns in the snow, the man pulled at the woolens wrapped around his face, pulling at them to give himself more air. His shouts had turned to sobs. Dulci caught a glimpse of a pale wind-chapped face and a bit of reddish-blond hair escaping his knit cap. His movements halted for a moment, as he gazed down into the snow, and Dulci felt a thrill of fear. *If I'm not crazy, who is this person? Why does he have blood on his hands? Why is he so upset?*

After a long moment, the man looked up. He gazed to Dulci's left, where the classroom windows had been. He reached up to unwind another wool scarf and Dulci saw his piercing blue eyes, looking strangely like... *No.* Dulci's eyes almost popped out of their sockets. This couldn't be...it looked like an older version of Finn!

Chapter 4

* * *

Dulci looked back at his hands, at his face. The man's brows loomed larger over his eyes than Finn's, but that was likely age and hardship. There was the same long straight nose with flaring nostrils, high forehead, square jaw: an older version of Finn MacDonald. He had his face screwed up in a grimace, and as she watched, he started moaning. Great sobs heaved out of him, and he fell to his knees, still clutching that last scarf.

Dulci gulped. A thousand thoughts ran through her head. *Am I crazy? Is he real? Where am I? And how do I get back to Normal Land?* She abruptly felt the bodhràn and tipper still in her hand, motionless all this time. She looked down. Did the drumming have something to do with this weird vision she was having? Should she try to talk to the guy? Only he looked so torn up about something...

When she looked up again from her bodhràn, she was looking out of Room 212's louvered windows. She glanced to the right. Mr. McKenna blinked, looking up from his violin. "Everything all right, Miss Oyselle?"

"I—there was—did I totally space out?"

"Well, no, that is, we were getting along swimmingly until that last key change I started. It's no bother, I can show you what the drum usually does when—"

"No, that's not it. I mean, something just happened, and I need to—" What did she need to do? It had seemed like ages but was probably only about thirty seconds. That was still longer than Mr. McKenna had said. What was going *on?* "I have to see someone. Sorry, I'll come back tomorrow, hopefully to explain. Can't stay now—bye!"

The memory of that reddish blonde hair, the liquid blue eyes, the wide forehead, the long, straight nose… she tried to block the pitiful expression from the face she had just started getting to know. She had to find Finn and make sure nothing terrible had happened to him.

* * *

Racing through the hallway, down the stairs, out across the back field to the place where the hockey team did their conditioning, she had to stop, shade her eyes against the late afternoon sun, and squint to see where Finn might be. Most of the team players were straggling in clumps running around the field, doing laps. How would she find him? What did he look like in a jersey? Where was that hair? There! He was running along the far right of the track, talking with one other runner as they went, his head turned away from her.

Dulci stopped and gulped to slow her breath, holding a hand to her side. *He's fine. Okay. So stop staring and turn around so that no one thinks you're a weirdo.* But as she turned to go back to the school building, the coach hailed her and was already jogging over. *Oh, God,* she thought. *What can I say I was doing?*

"Hey Dulci," Coach Johnson said. He was the owner of the clothing store downtown in Glace Cove, and had known her most of her life. "Anything wrong? You come with a message for one of the players or something?"

"No, Mr. Johnson. Sorry, I just—I was really worried something might have happened. But nothing did, so I'll just be going home now."

With that she turned and hot-footed it back to the

building, where she could still grab her backpack and apologize to Mr. McKenna. She walked more slowly up the stairs than she had raced down them, her mind turning back to the drum, the snow, the man, the blood. Was she seeing Finn's future? She shook the shiver from her spine that descended on that thought.

"Mr. McKenna?" she knocked on his still-open door. He was out, however, so she nipped in to grab her bag and get out of there. The room itself spooked her now, with no one there. She looked at the bodhràn on the chair and the violin in its case on the floor now, wondering. But she didn't want to talk to him just yet. She wanted to go home, calm down, maybe ask her parents what they thought it could be.

* * *

By the time she reached home, Dulci had outlined a sort of hypothesis to test. She thought her dad would appreciate that, being a scientist. For one thing, she could be going crazy. But if not, and what she'd seen was real, who was that guy? Was it really Finn in the future, and she was meant to warn him about something? And finally, how real was the whole thing? Was she in danger when she saw the vision? It had felt like she was actually there, on that snowy hillside, but she remembered her feet feeling glued into place, so maybe if she didn't move, she wasn't really there, and it was all in her mind? And what if the older Finn was able to see her? What then?

Stop, she thought sternly. *Stick to the four points: am I crazy, am I seeing the future, what's the purpose of seeing the future, and was I in danger when it happened, or immune? God, I hope Mom or Dad knows something about this.*

She opened the front door of her house and called out, "I'm home!" After a moment, she heard a muffled reply from the basement office where her dad worked. She poked her head into the stairwell, looking down to the corner of the jumbled space where an enormous desk held court next to the only source of heat, the furnace.

Her dad faced away, concentrating on typing up a last stray thought.

"Hey, Dad?"

"Mm-hmm, one second, Dulci."

"Is Mom home?"

"Uh-uh. Hang on."

Dulci cocked an ear to the rest of the house, and made sure her mom hadn't come home while her dad was too absorbed to notice, but no, she didn't hear any other creatures stirring. She waited a few more moments in silence. Finally, with a flourish of his hands to one side, and then a quick tap-tap to save his work, her dad turned around.

"Got it! Now what is it, *ma petite?* How was school?" He rose and walked toward the stairs.

"It was fine, but something really weird happened. I wanted to ask if you know what might have happened, like, scientifically."

"A science question? Sure, let's have it."

"Well," Dulci started. This was so weird. Would he even believe her? She hadn't even told him who Finn was yet. "Well," she started again. "I made this suggestion for a music club last week, on the first day of school, and Mr. McKenna asked me to stay behind to see what I played. I was drumming on the bodhràn he had at school, and—" Dulci swallowed hard. This wouldn't be so easy for her scientist father to take after all. "And I saw a vision of a man on a snowy hill, *in* the classroom, and it looked like Finn MacDonald, the new boy whose family just moved back here."

"What do you mean, 'saw a vision'? Was the song about a man in the snow?"

Dulci shook her head. "No, it had nothing to do with what I saw. It was a Bonnie Prince Charlie song, but what I saw was a man, climbing through snow, wiping the blood off his hands with the snow —"

"Blood?" His tone tone changed, sharpened abruptly.

"You saw someone wiping blood off his hands? In the classroom? This Mr. McKenna—was he—?"

"No, Dad, I'm trying to tell you—Mr. McKenna just disappeared! I was in the classroom drumming, when all of a sudden, I was freezing cold, on this snowy hill at night, and a man came up over the top of it, and he was all bundled up, but he unwrapped his hands to wipe them off, and unwrapped his face, and he looked so sad—"

"Dulci," his tone had changed again, to one of patient forbearance. "Are you just making this up? You know what you're saying sounds like a dream. A bad dream, but a dream. Have you even met this new boy Finn?"

"Yes. He actually asked me out on a date. I was going to ask you and Mom about that too," she said softly. *Had it been just a dream?*

"He asked you—well, that's great, Dulci. How old is this Finn?"

"He's a junior."

"And you said his name is MacDonald, and that his family used to live here. They're not the MacDonalds from out Baddeck way, are they?"

"How'd you know that?"

"We used to be in a supper club with them when your mom and I were first married. I'll be darned. That's great." His look of fond reminiscence shifted back to parental concern. "And don't you worry, I'm sure Finn's a good boy. His parents are good people, and his mom makes a killer spaghetti sauce, as I recall." He smiled, and Dulci tried to smile back. Now she had an answer to both questions: yes, she could go on the date, and yes, she was going crazy.

Chapter 5

* * *

The same time next day Dulci was in her room, staring at her own bodhràn, sitting on its wide shelf above her desk. She hadn't bothered to mention anything about the vision to her mother at dinner last night, and had even forborne spilling the beans to Mehron at school that day. She'd gone back to Mr. McKenna after school to let him know she'd just remembered someone she needed to check on urgently, and that it wouldn't happen again (although *who knew?* a voice whispered in her head).

She kept recalling that blistering cold wind she'd felt for those few moments, the shock of seeing a face whose structure she recognized as the that of Finn, the boy she liked. She gazed at the drum, the soft light filtering in from her upper window falling on it, lighting up the dust floating through the air. She wanted to be able to forget the episode altogether, put it behind her as a bad dream, like her father had said. But it had felt so *real*. And she hadn't been asleep.

Dulci took the few steps from her bed to the shelf and pulled down the bodhràn, catching the tipper as it fell out of its slot in the back. She looked out the window, leaned on the edge of her desk, and propped the drum up against her left hip. She waggled the tipper in the air a few times, then struck the middle of the stretched leather. A deep thud erupted, the echo of which she wiped away quickly with a fast rhythm in 4/4 time, sliding her arm forward and back across the leather, feeling the beat settle into her bones, her bones thrum with the instrument.

She looked out the window, but nothing was there save her ordinary view: the coastal road around town, curving past their house, the big maple tree in their front yard on its slope downward toward the bay, and the sea, grey-white and sparkling in the late sun.

She stopped abruptly. She could ask Joan Tebnek. Mehron's mom believed in visions, not only because Jesse's illness had no other explanation, but because her family seemed to have a history of them. Neither she nor Mehron saw things, but tales had come down that she had occasionally shared with the girls when they were little and interested in ghost stories. Well, Mehron had been interested; Dulci had tried not to listen, as they kept her awake at night.

She grabbed her parka from its hook and pattered down the stairs to yell towards the basement door: "I'm going over to Mehron's!" She got an answering "Okay!" before reaching the front door, which she opened and closed carefully. Then she was off at a run, down the coastal road, following it to its end.

* * *

She didn't run far before stopping from the stitch in her side, and continuing at a walk. She placed her hands on her head the way she'd seen Mehron do at soccer matches when they were younger. Now it was all about basketball, which would mean she'd still be at school. She could talk to Joan without worrying about Mehron's reaction. She was Dulci's best friend, but sometimes she was just too practical. She wanted someone who believed in things they couldn't see.

She got to the Mi'kmaq settlement on the south edge of town and turned a sharp left off the road, almost doubling back to skip through the gated entrance. It was never closed, day or night, whenever she'd visited. She walked faster past the old teepee used for ceremonies and living history exhibits, and found the Tebneks' house at the end of the street facing up the hill, away from the water. Her knock took almost a minute to be answered, but as they had no bell, and Joan might be busy, she waited before knocking again, since that would have been rude.

"Dulci! Well. What a pleasant surprise, come on in. I'm just finishing up on a genealogy project for someone before starting supper, so I'm spread all over the table…"

Dulci stepped into the hug Joan offered, then turned to close the door and follow her through the pokey hallway to the kitchen, the heart of every house but especially this one. She followed the broad back, covered today in a pale pink cotton pique dress with long patterned sleeves in flannel. Dulci had asked many times where her mom got her clothes, but Mehron always said it was just a combination of 'found, made, and gussied-up.' Dulci liked it. It was such a contrast to Olive's starched polyester and wool, in beiges and browns and navy.

Joan turned around as they reached the table, showing Dulci her tanned face, her shiny black hair drawn into two braids, and her snapping black eyes. She was the only one in the family who 'went traditional,' in the Mi'kmaq way. Mehron with her sports and boys, Tuotu with his scientific equipment and lab qualifications; they left Joan to keep up the cultural heritage of their family, which drew Dulci even more to her, as that was the sort of thing she wished to do for her own family, someday.

Dulci looked at the kitchen table: it was indeed strewn with all manner of papers and envelopes, photos and certificates. She sat down, careful not to upset the piles, as Joan cleared them away into their respective folders. "Now what brings you here so early? Mehron won't be done with practice for another forty minutes, you know."

"I know. Actually, I wanted to talk to you, Joan." Joan looked up at that and gave a little moue of bashfulness; Dulci felt heartened. "It's about a vision I had yesterday."

"A vision, you say? Did you talk to your parents about it? I don't want to go interfering with what they say."

"I tried to talk to Dad about it, but he said it was just a bad dream. But I can't seem to get it out of my mind, and I can't help but think it was more than that."

"Hmm, I see."

"And I didn't bother telling Mom about it, because she'd just say the same thing."

"Mm-hmm."

"But I thought you might be—you might have a different point of view—you might understand, because of Jesse…"

"Ah, that's it," Joan said softly. "That may be true. Let's hear it then." She'd stopped putting away the papers and sat next to Dulci at the four-person table. She looked straight ahead as Dulci wound through her tale, the same as she had yesterday with her dad. But she didn't interrupt as he had, and seemed to be envisioning what she described. A shiver went up Dulci's spine at the thought.

She described the way she'd come back from the vision, with a blast of wind pushing from behind and turning to see Mr. McKenna only just turning to look at her. It reminded Dulci of the Narnia tales, when the Professor said it was very likely Lucy was telling the truth precisely because no time had seemed to pass while she was in that other world for ages. "Well, what do you think, Joan? Am I going crazy? Or am I—am I a Seer?"

Joan turned toward Dulci, keeping her gaze down and thoughtful. "Well, Dulci, I don't know. I don't think one vision is enough to call you crazy. But I bet you're the only one who will ever know what the vision was about. If you don't know now, it may need some more time to make sense, that's all."

Dulci pondered that. It showed Finn when he was

older, so maybe she would stay friends with him until then, or they might even get married, and she would need to know about this possibility—this moment in his future — in order to protect him from something. That sort of made sense. "But *who* is sending me the visions? And am I supposed to do something about them now? Or just wait?"

"I don't know. Like I said, that is for only you to decide. Let me tell you a story about Imkaniji, one of the Keskimsit, who are like one of your Seers, those who see layers of the future. She said they were like reflections of reflections, seen through onionskins. She was never sure when a vision would take place, but depending on the circumstance, she would act on what she thought the Spirits were trying to tell her when they gave her these glimpses. There have been several Keskimsit, or specially gifted people, in our history, but Imkaniji is the one we most closely associated with our Glace Cove band."

Dulci fiddled with the zipper on her coat as she listened to the Imkaniji story, but didn't see that it told her what to do in her own situation. She sighed. Joan moved to touch her forearm, and looked her in the eye.

"The Mi'kmaq stories of Seers are mostly about women, too, you know. They were trusted by Kisúlkw with the power to see. And the men trusted them to use it wisely. Sometimes white women had this power, but then they were not trusted by their own people. They called them witches. But I think you learned about them, right?"

A small smile crept into Joan's voice as she glanced up at Dulci, who nodded. They'd studied the witch trials that took place in America, where the Puritans had tortured women when they couldn't understand the medicine they practiced or the beliefs they held. People were more sensible here in Canada, more measured in their judgements even then, so they thought. *Except when they see snow in a second-floor classroom on a clear autumn day*, thought Dulci wryly. "So the Mi'kmaq women who were Seers, they just did what they thought the visions told them?"

"No, that's not what I said," Joan said, almost irritated, as a loud bang signaled that Mehron was home from practice.

"Hey!" came the pleased shout as Mehron came in from the hallway and stopped short at sight of Dulci. Tuotu followed soon after, whistling. He hung his coat on the peg and stretched his long arms in his green-checked flannel shirt.

"Hey yourself," she replied. "I was just asking your mom some questions about a school assignment." Joan looked at her with some surprise, and Dulci felt a little guilty. Didn't she know her daughter would totally make fun of her for fantasizing about Finn when they hadn't even been on their date yet? She was a champion at teasing, and always got the better of Dulci.

"Oh—well, you gonna stay for dinner then?"

"Oh no, I don't need to, my dad was home when I came over—"

"Come on, you should stay. You can help me with my Stupid Math homework."

"It's not Stupid Math—" Joan started up.

"I know," replied Mehron, "but it's light years behind what Dulci's working on. Please?"

"Ok, just let me call and check." Dulci went over to the kitchen phone on the wall and dialed her own home number. Her mom answered on the fourth ring. She okayed Dulci staying for dinner, and just asked if she needed to swing by to pick her up afterwards. "No," Tuotu piped up, deducing the question from her side of the conversation. "I'll drive her back up the road." It's not that it was far or dangerous—Dulci walked down it all the time—but after dark, two miles was a long walk. Besides that, it was near the sea, which was known to cause its own share of accidents.

That decided, Dulci settled in with the three Tebneks for dinner. Joan dished out the pan-fried fish, and her homemade tomato sauce and spiced rice lay on a TV tray table next to the main table. Joan made a fake groan as Tuotu reached to the top of the refrigerator to pull down a half-full bag of potato chips. Mehron's face lit up. Dulci knew this was a long-standing war, and that Tuotu always wheedled his way into winning. After a couple sporting comments shot back and forth, Tuotu returned the winning sally: "But it's a vegetable!"

Dulci giggled and shook her head as the others smiled at the never-failing line.

Just then, another loud noise interrupted their cozy dinner chat. It was the door again, but not its opening and closing. Had something fallen onto the front door? Tuotu half-rose, waiting to see if there was any other sound. It came again, this time accompanied by a loud moan. At the human sound, Joan's eyes closed in a reserved stillness, and Tuotu muttered something that Dulci couldn't make out. "What is it?" Dulci whispered to Mehron, seated next to her at the kitchenette. "Just Jesse," Mehron mumbled, trying to sound dismissive, but her worry showed through.

Before Tuotu made it around the table to the hallway, the front door blew open and a howling wind tore through the hallway into the warm kitchen. Jesse tumbled through with it, propelled by its force. His dad caught him before he knocked over the table with all the food, but he very nearly upended the pot with the steaming tomato sauce. Joan let out a breath as Tuotu led Jesse away, unseeing, into the living room to lay him on the sofa. Dulci had seen his eyes: wild.

Jesse was tall, but Tuotu was still taller, and bulkier, thank goodness, or else Jesse might have hurt himself. He was talking to himself in a jumble, in words Dulci could hear but not understand. She looked down at her plate, the good mood drained from the kitchen as effectively as the warm air had been sucked out of it. She felt awkward, since Jesse had been at special facilities or kept at home for four years, and she hardly knew him anymore. She glanced at Mehron, and saw that she was stabbing at the fish on her plate, stuffing it into her mouth, heedless of her own pulse racing under her jaw.

Joan's face was more resigned, it seemed to Dulci. She knew it must still hurt each time one of Jesse's fits happened. And Tuotu?

Tuotu was looking at her with an apology in his face. "It doesn't usually take him when he's walking to and from places, you know, Dulci. We thought that was a safe activity. But ever since a week ago, right before the ship got back, it's gotten worse. We don't know what to do."

Dulci looked at Joan again. She swallowed awkwardly. "I'm really sorry. I wish he could go back to how he was before. Is there anything that helps?"

"Not being around people," Tuotu volunteered. "That's what he was at all summer, avoiding people and finding peace in nature." His gaze returned to the living room doorway. "But..."

Dulci put the bite of fish she'd been holding into her mouth. She couldn't taste it. She put down her fork. "Maybe I should go home now?" Tuotu sighed, and nodded.

"It tasted really good, Joan. Sorry I couldn't—"

Joan just shook her head, dismissing her fumbling apology. "You just let me know if you have any more questions about—about that school project, okay?" Her eyes sought and held Dulci's for a serious moment, then dropped away. "Always good to have you over."

Tuotu rose to get his jacket and car keys, and Dulci saw Joan place his plate in the oven to stay warm. They got in his truck in silence, and stayed quiet all the short trip back to the Oyselles' place. Tuotu turned to Dulci in the passenger seat, a world of defeated dreams in his expression, and the question of whether she'd understand in his eyes. "It'll be okay, Tuotu," she said, and vaulted down from the high cab.

As she waved Tuotu down the steep driveway, Dulci stayed in the yard a moment, feeling the dark, the chill, of the northern autumnal night. And something else: something bearing down on her.

She drew a deep breath and blew it out in slow, measured beats. She was taking something on, she could feel it. If she accepted that she was a Seer, she had to decide how to help Finn with what she had seen. If her parents didn't believe her, that was fine. At least Joan Tebnek did. She wondered what Finn himself might say about it.

Chapter 6

* * *

Saturday. The day of her date with Finn. Her first date. Dulci woke up like normal, with her blankets twisted around her legs and her book squashed under her pillow, but then she remembered. Immediately she felt her stomach go into knots and her back tense up. What was she going to say to him? She'd managed to tell him on Friday that yes, she could go out that weekend, and avoided him the rest of the school day.

She had two main worries. First, should she tell him about the vision? She felt he should know, since it was about him, but she didn't want to give him the impression she went around dreaming of him…ugh! She'd have to just wait and see if he seemed trustworthy. And second, what did a girl bloody *do* on a first date with a guy she hardly knew? She had asked Mehron in a roundabout way, but hadn't gotten anything good. Since Mehron had been on dates with guys she'd known all her life, they already had common ground to stand on, whereas she and Finn didn't know each other, except that she thought she'd glimpsed him in a weird, ghostly future. Dulci exhaled in frustration. It was going to be awkward, she just knew it.

She'd taken a shower, braided her hair, and dressed in her newest, and coolest—she hoped—clothes. She wondered where he would take her for lunch, since he hadn't lived here long enough to have gotten around and seen much yet. Probably the Bar and Grill on the water. Or maybe Sharon's diner, off the high street. Her stomach fluttered. Her phone read 9:12. She needed something to do to pass the time.

She didn't dare start drumming when she was thinking about Finn so hard. All right then, a little bit of breakfast, so I'm not starving when he gets here. She went downstairs to find her dad still at the dining room table, leaning motionless over the newspaper.

"Hey Dad," she said. "Is Mom still home?"

He spoke without moving his head. "Morning, Dulci. No, her car's gone. I think she's over at the MacIntyres' about a deposition. Why, did you need something?" His head came up at his last question.

"No, just wondering. I'm all ready to go, but I have some time to wait. Bored, I guess."

"Bored? My Dulci, on a Saturday morning like this?" She could tell he was teasing, but didn't feel like taking the bait.

"I guess I'll grab some granola and do some reading," she said. She went back to the kitchen, hearing her dad's comment, "Well, if you are bored, I can think of a few things for you to do," and ignoring it.

She made up her super-duper granola, which started with the cereal box, then went on to include blueberries, chopped apple, and her aunt's special pecans from down south. She dolloped on the yogurt and then went to find a book that would either distract her or calm her spirits. She stood in front of the tall barrister's bookcase that stood on the stairway landing for several minutes, but nothing from her father's naturalist collection was feeling right. Back up to her own bedroom, where she scanned the low shelves that wrapped under her window seat. A-ha! She pulled out an illustrated travel book, one that told of a woman's adventures around the world, and proceeded down the stairs again with its big spine tucked under her arm.

She snuggled into the window seat in the living room, where there was both a cushion and a nearby lamp. Too bad it was so late in the morning and no sunlight came through. Dulci sighed and dug into her gourmet granola, balancing the big book on her knees and cradling her bowl in her lap. She read of far-off places like Kazakhstan, Burma, Tunisia, and the Carribbean, each chapter highlighting a particular conversation or person that the author had found fascinating and compelling. Dulci dreamed of being in those places, having her own adventures. Who was to say that she couldn't blaze her own adventure trail?

She finished the bowl and it went on the floor beside the seat. She gazed at one particular photo: it was a group of three Burmese women, all in fancy dress, shiny headpieces and painted hands. One was looking at the other two. One was looking down at the table with a slight smile on her face as she ground up something in a mortar. And the third was looking at the camera, mischievous delight in her eyes, her long fingers wrapped round a blue bowl, held out to the picture-taker. Nothing in the text explained the picture, it was just a photo of daily life, maybe, or a hostess preparing something for the author. But something about the energy and vividness of the group entranced Dulci. She wished she could have a job that took her to places and people like that: different, lively, fascinating.

A door slammed in the front of the house and Dulci jumped. She heard the clatter of the coat tree taking a coat and umbrella: must be her mother come back from her errand. She put down the book, bussed her bowl to the sink where she could rinse it out, then saw that it was all crusty. *Have to let it soak now,* she thought, annoyed. "Hey, Mom."

Olive swooped into the kitchen, without her trademark trench coat, but still in a silk blouse, pearls, and wool trousers. She always dressed as if she was an extra on *Leave It To Beaver.* "Morning, Dulci. Are you just up? You look like you're still asleep."

Dulci did still feel a little entranced by her traveling thoughts, but quickly shook them off to answer. "No, I've been up for hours, I've just been waiting around for —" Before she could finish, the doorbell rang. Cold panic flooded Dulci's core. *Oh, shit,* she thought, but said to her mother, "Could you answer that? And just give me two minutes?" and bolted for the stairs. She rushed to stand before her full-length mirror. She saw her straight, brown hair, parted on the side and meekly staying in its braid; her pale face and pointy chin eclipsed by the deep-set dark eyes; the slouchy green sweatshirt she'd chosen because of its illegible scrawl—she figured Finn wouldn't be able to read it and just think it artistic; the black skinny jeans that made her legs look like toothpicks, but were okay since they gave her a derriere; the green Converse she had just barely managed to buy from her allowance when her mother refused to buy them. She looked as good as she knew how. *Well, here we go then.*

* * *

Finn was waiting for her on the couch in the living room, smiling at her mother, when she came down five minutes later. He stood up, his smile broadening, when he saw her. Something that wasn't butterflies fluttered near Dulci's stomach, and she smiled back at him.

"Hey, Finn. Sorry to keep you waiting—I got lost reading for a while. Ready now."

"No problem. I just got to meet your mom." He turned to Olive. "Nice meeting you, Mrs. Oyselle. I'm sure we'll talk about the circuit court system again soon," he said with a reassuring, cocky grin. Dulci recoiled a little. Maybe she wouldn't be telling him about the vision, if he was going to turn all oily salesman. Finn turned back to her. "Ready?"

Something did a flip under her ribcage. The oily salesman was gone and there was something vulnerable in his expression, Dulci thought. *How does he do that?* "Yep, let's go. Bye, Mom."

Olive didn't respond except to raise a hand as the two filed out the front door. Dulci and Finn walked down the steep driveway to where Finn had parked his car, a large, old, pickup truck in a faded blue. He unlocked her door and opened it for her, then walked round to the driver's side and got in himself. They cruised down to the main street a minute before either spoke, and only when Finn had pulled over to the curb did he ask her, "So where would you like to go for lunch?"

Dulci was a little taken aback. *I thought that was his job? Now I have to think of somewhere good? Unfair!* Her mind reeled back to the options in town. Then she looked at Finn. "Have you been to the Bell shops yet?"

"No, where're those?"

"I'll show you how to get there. It's a ways out of town, like 10 minutes. Is that okay?"

"A'course. Just don't get me lost!" He grinned.

Dulci directed him just fine; there were only a few turnings to get to the little shopping arcade on the big inland lake, the Bras-d'Or. It housed a candy shop, a deli, a comic-and-bookstore, and, of all things, a wax museum.

"They do really good soups and sandwiches," Dulci explained, pointing to the sign that read "All Points Bulletin Deli and Cafe" in black on white. "Also hot chocolate." She eyed Finn as she said that, hoping he wouldn't think hot chocolate was a kid thing to drink—she hated coffee—and was pleased to see his eyes light up with appreciation. "Sounds good," he said.

A few minutes were spent perusing the menu and admiring the view of the lake. Then they lapsed into an awkward silence.

Everything floating through Dulci's brain seemed hopelessly lame. *Do you think you'll have a good school year? Do you like it here? Have you met many people yet? What are your hobbies?* She kicked herself for letting the silence continue. Finally, Finn spoke.

"So you like hot chocolate. Is it your favorite drink?" He looked at her with that open expression that gave her goosebumps. She decided to be herself.

"Yes. I don't like coffee, but tea's okay. What about you?" It was a beginning.

They skittered around several topics. Dulci discovered he liked cars, he hoped to join the hockey team, and he had ridden in rodeos when his family lived near Calgary. She told him that she liked reading, and drumming, and then wished she didn't sound like such an anti-social homebody. Their soups and sandwiches came and were quickly scarfed down. *At least I don't have to worry about eating like a lady in front of him*, Dulci thought with a chuckle.

"So it's not drumming like in a band? You drum with fiddles and tin whistles?"

"Yes, and sometimes flutes or pipes, which is even better. It's a drum from Irish folk music, actually." Dulci warmed to her subject. "I've only been to a few live concerts, when Dad has taken me out to a Celtic Colours festival performance, or we've gone down to Halifax for a weekend. And I've played in ceilidhs a couple times, but only with older folks after church. I get most of my practice time listening to videos online and playing along. Playing on my own can get boring." She remembered the news that related to this tidbit.

"But there's going to be a club at school, which should be cool! I just met with Mr. McKenna on Friday —" her voice faltered.

Finn picked up on that immediately, since he was studying her so intently. Why was he doing that? "I haven't heard of him, is he one of the teachers at school then?"

"Yes," she said slowly. "He teaches some of the higher math classes and the music electives. I wrote a suggestion and put it into the box on the first day of school, so he called me in to ask about what kind of music I was interested in. He thinks there's a good chance that there are others with a Celtic music background who would like to join in." Her spirits picked up again. "It should be fun, but—" Finn waited. "But something happened while I was meeting with him. Something really, really weird. I'm not even sure I should tell you—"

Finn's eyebrows shot up. "He didn't—"

"No! No, it had nothing to do with Mr. McKenna. Nothing bad like that. It was something I saw. I just don't want you to think I'm crazy." She looked down at the detritus of cold fries and parsley garnishes on their plates, waiting for the right words and the right decision to tell her what to do. At that moment the server came around to ask if they needed anything else. *Yes, God, yes, tell me what to do*, Dulci thought, but no answer came. As soon as she'd departed with the dishes, Dulci sighed. She looked up at Finn.

"What do you know about the Second Sight?"

"Second sight? Like seeing the future and stuff? Not much, except that it runs in my family."

"It—what? It runs in your family? Do you have visions of the future then?"

"Not me, thank goodness. Those people always seem a little, well, sad. Like, weighed down. They keep to themselves, at least the ones in my family did." As he talked, Finn's demeanor changed; he looked down and seemed less at ease.

"My mom's pretty normal, she's the one that runs the online business. They sell art prints, mugs, t-shirts, stuff like that, but the Canadian supplier got too expensive and they didn't want to shift to China—anyway." He broke off, embarrassed. "That's why we moved here. Cheaper. But my dad, he's… he gets depressed sometimes. Mom thought it would be better for him to come back here…"

He shifted in his seat and flicked his eyes up at Dulci instead of meeting her gaze. Dulci took this in, and decided to tell him anyway.

"Well, I've never had this happen before, but I think that I had a vision with the Sight." She took a breath. "And you were in it."

His eyes changed. From possibly troubled, they narrowed to keen engagement. "Me?" A hungry curiosity in his tone.

"Yeah, or an older version of you."

"An older—like my dad? What'd I do? What'd I say? Did I talk to you?"

"You seemed—" *How should I break this to him?* "—Very sad. You were walking through the snow, all bundled up, and it sounded like moaning, but when you unwrapped the muffler over your face, it was—it was crying. Then you shouted something over the hill, but I don't know what. And then I was back in the classroom. It was beyond strange, like I was somewhere else entirely."

There were several moments of silence as Finn took this in. Dulci felt the vision again: the chill in the wind, the swish of the leather boots in the snowdrift. It came to her through the sounds of the cafe, the steam shrieking from the espresso machine, the beep of the register as other customers were rung up. She opened her eyes, which she didn't know she'd closed, and gazed out the window next to their table, the view a long one over the lake, with mountains rising on the far shore like sleeping forms turned away from the sun.

"Well, I don't think you're crazy. It happens in my family," Finn said. "But I've never had someone see *me*." He blew out a tense breath and looked her in the eye. "Or someone like me. That's interesting, actually, seeing as how you'd only just met me. Maybe I made a really good impression?" The twinkle in his eye told her he was kidding, but Dulci didn't feel like giving in to the teasing.

"Or maybe I'm supposed to help you." She wished it

unsaid as soon as it was out of her mouth but couldn't take it back. Instead, she looked down, sweeping imaginary crumbs off the table to the floor. "Anyways, I don't know much of anything about the Sight. Why don't you tell me more about your family history?"

"Well, there's two instances I know of, that my dad always told me stories of when I was little," he started, more comfortable now. "The first was my dad's aunt, whom I never met. She died just after my parents were married, before I was born. My dad says she would often go into little trances, and people thought she was a bit daft, but she told him it was just her reflecting on life, and being 'better connected to those who passed' that did it." Finn turned from the window to look at Dulci. He grinned. "Sound about right?"

He didn't expect a response, and continued more somberly. "The other story was about a way-back Mac-Donald, the first one who came here from Scotland, like two hundred years ago. He was said to have a lot of bad luck here in Cape Breton, and finally emigrated out south to the Great Lakes for work. He married and had children, obviously—" Here he pulled a face for Dulci. "—but he didn't do very well. The family didn't prosper on Lake Superior and ended up going further west into the plains of Saskatchewan, building a house in one of the new settlements there. My dad took me to see it a few years ago. The descendants are sprinkled all across Ontario and the plains. My great-aunt, the one I told you about, was the first one to come back to Cape Breton. My grandpa moved back some time after, but then he died, when I was really little."

Finn's voice got softer. "My dad says he had stories of this ancestor having the Sight when he was moving from Cape Breton to the Lakes and then the plains, and that he turned into a ghost."

Dulci felt frozen to the seat. *A ghost? Why?* Is that what she'd seen, instead of a potential future? A frisson of unease shivered down her spine and she shook slightly.

"What? You don't like ghost stories?" Finn was teasing again. "Should we get some hot chocolate then before we go back? I'd like to see what the best hot chocolate around here tastes like."

She smiled faintly, and nodded. He went to order them from the front counter. He came back, sat, and reached across the table with his palms up. "Dulci," he looked at her seriously. "I don't think you're crazy. I can believe in things I don't see. And maybe you *are* meant to help me."

Dulci cringed at her own words, but saw that he meant to be friendly, and cautiously placed a hand in his.

"I didn't know if I should tell you this either," Finn said, leaning in closer. "But when you passed me in the hall that first day, I felt something… strange, too. When I looked into your eyes for that half a second. Like I was a magnet and you were the fridge." He grinned sheepishly at his own metaphor, and Dulci squeezed his hand. "I mean, not that you weren't cute and everything, I do think you're pretty, it's just—there was an extra feeling too." He was *blushing!*

Dulci felt a bubbling up of happiness and gave him a genuine smile. Who cared if it was kind of a weird first date? He had commented on her eyes, those pale green-gray eyes she was always wishing were stronger, more intense.

He was nervous too. Plus, he had Seers in his family. That was enough to make her relax on her two accounts. The hot chocolates arrived, topped with whipped cream. As they dove in, Dulci laughed and teased him right back.

Chapter 7

* * *

After believing she'd never fall asleep that night, Dulci was out like a light. She woke up on Sunday with eyes open wide and an electric feeling. She had to go to Mehron's house!

A glance out her window told her that it was overcast and the wind was blowing in gusts off the bay. She texted Mehron to say she was coming down to dish about the date, and Mehron said OK, she was up. She hopped into warm clothes, serviceable ones as opposed to the stylish ones from yesterday, and pounded down the stairs in her usual way. Her dad asked where she was going, at eight o'clock on a Sunday, then told her to be back for lunch. She yelled back at him that she would and tripped out the door and down the road, slowing quickly to an energetic walk, not able to contain the nervous energy that made her a bit giddy.

She got to their front door at 8:28 AM, and gave a smart rap on the door, waiting breathlessly. A long moment passed with no sound from inside. Dulci checked her phone again. No other texts; Mehron should at least be up and able to answer the door. She knocked again, a little more tentatively. She'd barely pulled away her hand when the door was thrust out. Jesse confronted her, his smooth face paler than it should be, contrasting with his tufty black hair. He looked like he'd just woken up, and was in a bad mood, blinking at her and the thin sunlight before standing back to allow her to pass through. She walked in, feeling his form loom over her by a good six inches, smelling like old clothes and leather. She wrinkled her nose, and scampered through to the kitchen, where Mehron was sitting over a bowl of cereal.

She sat down across the table from her as she heard Jesse noisily find his way back to his bedroom. Ignoring it, she turned to Mehron, whose face held a sly smile. It quickly turned to a grin as she saw Dulci's face light up with anticipation. "Soooo… how was it?"

"It was nice. My first date was nice," replied Dulci. She punctuated this statement with a prim nod. This set Mehron giggling. "Aaaand… details, come on!"

"Well, there were some awkward pauses, actually it was really awkward at first…" Dulci launched into a play-by-play from the moment he knocked on her door. Mehron didn't interrupt, but supplied appropriate squeals, guffaws, and eye rolls. Dulci left out the fact that she'd had a vision with *him* in it, but she included his mention of Second Sight in his family. She was just about to get to the highlight, when he'd called her 'pretty,' when another crash sounded from beyond the kitchen door. Jesse appeared in the doorframe, still bleary, still scruffy, and proceeded to open the fridge and stare inside. With barely a pause for the interruption, Dulci continued her tale.

"And he called me *pretty*, right before he said there was some *magnetism* when he saw me before that first assembly. Isn't that totally sweet? I think it was—"

Before she could finish her thought, Jesse had barged in on their conversation again. He leaned over to slam his hands none-too-gently on the table between Mehron and Dulci. The rickety frame screeched. His eyes locked on Dulci's, and she saw an anger burning in them, competing with a lift of the inside of his eyebrows that signaled fear.

"You can't, go out, with that dude," he ground out.

"*Dude?* What are you talking about?" Dulci replied indignantly.

"You can't, go out with, a MacDonald." His breathing even seemed labored. *Jesus*, thought Dulci, *has he really gone totally batshit crazy?*

"Jesse—" Mehron started, but was silenced by the sharp shake of his head in her direction.

"You need, to stay away, from him." His eyebrows went up again, as if he was scared by what he saw in her face. *This is totally freaking me out*, thought Dulci. She stared him down, not trusting herself to reply with any more useful words, and after another moment he lurched back to the counter to grab the package of beef jerky he'd come for, then slammed back into his room.

Dulci looked round to Mehron with a wide-eyed, questioning look. The silence in the house now made her want to make some noise. Mehron glanced down, interested in her cereal bowl intensely once more. "Don't worry about him," she muttered. "He's probably just crazy." Even though her eyes remained on her bowl, Dulci sensed this dismissal of her only brother cost her a lot.

"No luck then with the new treatments?"

"Nope. Like this since the week before Dad got home. He barely eats. Just sleeps a lot. And causes a ruckus," she added, her voice pitched extra low. "He has an appointment with the psychiatrist for medications this week. Mom doesn't want to do it, but Dad says it's the only way he can grow out of it, or something like that."

"I'm sorry, Mehron. I wish I could help." Dulci's words sounded hollow, but it was all she could think of to say. Another short silence ensued, before Mehron heaved a sigh and asked, "So when's the next date?"

Chapter 8

* * *

Back home, Dulci sat in front of her desk, her legs propped up on its surface, her stockinged feet crossed at the ankle. She looked up at her bodhràn, zoning out. *Why can't I tell Mehron, but I can tell Joan?*

Because Joan believes in the magic of her own tribe, but Mehron totally doesn't. The answer came to her as she remembered images from the past with Mehron. Leaning over museum displays, Mehron scoffing; attending Mi'kmaq heritage days when there was a shaman telling stories, Mehron rolling her eyes; Joan letting slip that Jesse might be seeing visions to Tuotu when they didn't know she was there, Mehron's face a hard little chip of caramel brown ice. *No, Mehron wouldn't believe me if I told her.*

She felt unsteady as she stared at her drum, a vague thrill of the unknown unsettling her in this safest of places. Would there be more visions? Or was she done? Would she find out more about Finn? Or would images of others ricochet off her as she got older? Could she control when she had one? Like, if she started drumming quietly now…

But no, she wouldn't. She didn't know the purpose of the vision yet. She would wait to see if it happened again. Maybe it was just a dream, after all, or a one-off, a fluke.

If that was the way of it, she could get back to being just an ordinary girl. An ordinary girl who was going out with a totally cool junior, that is. *That part's not so bad*, she thought, before groaning aloud. She kicked her feet off the desk and turned round to pull out from her bag the books she needed for a homework assignment.

* * *

She yawned and stretched as she reread her last answer to the world history question. *Yeah, that's good enough*, she thought, and closed the book with a satisfying thunk. She moved to get her pajamas out of the dresser and changed, finishing with the fuzzy socks from last Christmas since the wind was still kicking about outside, had even picked up since she'd gotten home. She turned off the light and climbed into bed, glancing outside for the familiar street light and its little circle of street, lawn and sidewalk. What she saw was complete blackness.

She quickly fumbled for her lamp and turned the light back on. *Not a power outage.* She peered out again, her hand on the switch to click it forward twice to turn it off. Instead of a streetlight's pool of light she saw a small cloud of light, wavering behind a wisp of fog. The fog blew away and she saw a torch—two torches—blazing yellow, illuminating a scene below her window. Two men faced each other as if in a wrestling match. One was wrapped up like that older 'Finn' she'd seen before.

Oh God, it's another vision. The other man was shorter, slighter, and not as bundled up. The light of the torch illuminated long brown arms, only partially covered by rough suede jacket, even though there was snow on the ground beneath their feet. He wore a fur vest around his body, and two ornaments: a leather thong on one wrist, a beaded bracelet with two porcupine quills hanging from the other.

The Scotsman's hands were bare and red from the cold, but she could see no blood on them now. The Indian's hands were empty but held up in front of him. Dulci could see only his back, as he faced the bigger man. She felt frozen again, rooted to the floor of her bedroom, but she almost leapt forward when she saw the Scot make a move to swipe at the Indian. *He must have a knife. What is going on?* Dulci screamed inwardly, waiting for some sign or an outcome that would allow her to move.

It came when the Scotsman hesitated in his next stroke. In that moment, Dulci felt the air in her room change: as if it had been completely still before, but was now being sucked out by some breeze. She glanced at the window: still closed. She looked back at the scene outside: gone. She turned and ran down the stairs, through the house to the back door, and across the yard in her fuzzy socks. No snow. Just crackling leaves from the maple tree next to the house.

The streetlight illuminated the paved street, the sidewalk, and part of the hill coming up to her house. It was still except for the motion of the water against the rocks, a periodic swooshing that Dulci had always found comforting. Not now. She wanted to shout out names, call to the people she had seen, but they were just—gone.

That Mi'kmaq Indian wasn't from the future. What if I'm seeing the past?

* * *

Dulci sat in her room again, her hand once again on the lamp switch by her bed. She hesitated before turning it off, turning things over in her mind.

What if it's the past?
Then it's not about Finn.
Or is it?
Who was that Indian then?
Why is this happening to me?
What can I do to make it stop?
Do I need to tell someone—is that what I'm meant to do with this?

She thought about that one. If she told her dad, he'd think she was having delusions or getting boy-crazy or something. Send her to a therapist probably. If she told her mom, she'd give her that *look*, the one that plainly said, *Come on now, we're a bit too old for that.* If she told Joan? Well, Joan believed her, but didn't know what it *meant.* Maybe this second vision would mean something to her. It involved one of her own people, at least.

So, I'll definitely tell Joan. Tomorrow, after school. But what about Mehron?

Why was it just as difficult to think of telling Mehron as it was her parents? She was her best friend. They'd known each other for six years, grown up together through some hard times at school. Because Mehron is so *normal,* came the answer. She won't want to be wrapped up in any more weirdness than she has to, with her brother already going off the deep end. She wants to make new friends too, Dulci acknowledged with a pang. *I wouldn't want to make her look like the weird girl, with high school just starting.*

Dulci sighed. She would just have to talk to Joan tomorrow. And keep an eye out for other visions, since it wasn't just the drumming that called them up. The thought of having one during class made her stomach freeze up. She didn't want to be the weird girl either. I'm not going crazy. *There's an explanation here. A point. Somewhere.*

With that, she clicked off the light and stared out into the night. The streetlight flickered briefly back at her.

Chapter 9

*   *   *

The next school day flew by.

When she wasn't spacing out, thinking of the way the big Scot had swiped at the Indian outside her house, she was staring at the teacher, willing herself not to have a vision.

By the time she got to science class where Mehron sat waiting for her, she felt worn out, her nerves like they'd been danced upon. *Three more classes,* she told herself.

When she didn't say anything to Mehron, just offered a weak smile, Mehron leaned over. "I'm sorry about yesterday. Maybe I should start coming over to your house instead, so he doesn't bother us."

Dulci looked up, her reverie broken. "Oh, it's no big deal. Don't worry about it. But yeah, you can come over if you want. Dad's always in the basement and Mom's usually out."

Mehron seemed about to say something else when the teacher started talking. They both opened their books, looking down obediently.

* * *

When the bell rang for the end of her last class— thank goodness they'd had to watch a safety video instead of suiting up for P.E.—Dulci packed up her things and

49

walked straight out the front doors toward the center of town. The library wasn't far, and she'd checked online to make sure Joan was holding one of her office hours as town historian there.

When she entered the library, passing its two small stone lions and walking round to the reference desk, she saw Joan Tebnek seated, her gaze on a computer screen to her right. She looked over at Dulci's entrance and smiled.

"Ah, Dulci, nice to see you. What's up? Anything I can do for you today?"

"Hi, Joan. Um…" God, this was worse than having to tell her mom she'd gotten her period. "I, um, had another one of those visions. And I don't think it's the future I'm seeing."

Joan's face instantly became longer and more serious and she let go the smile. "How do you know?"

"This one I had last night had the same guy, but also a guy who was dressed in the old Mi'kmaq costume, with suede and fur and the beaded bracelet and everything." She gulped.

"I see." Joan's eyes watched Dulci for a moment before looking down, then over at her computer screen. She looked back at Dulci. "And what do you want to ask me about?"

"Well, they didn't seem very—friendly, to one another." Dulci pulled a wry smile. "I was wondering if you knew of any feuds or fights, like personal, individual ones. In the 1800s. During winter." At Joan's quirked brow, Dulci added, "There's been snow both times, big piles of it."

"Hmm. Well, that's pretty specific, but we normally only see records of the conflicts that a lot of people were involved in, not the squabbles between families. Like this, for example." She turned her computer screen so Dulci could see.

There were several application screens open. On the

left was a black and white picture of a birchbark wigwam and two Mi'kmaq women in front of it. Behind the wigwam, something was smoking. On the upper right of the monitor, a window showed some old typeface, maybe an old newspaper announcement. It said in large letters, "Indian Sets Fire to Town Hall." In the window on the lower right, there was a bulleted list, and Dulci saw only a few lines—charges of arson, brothers away to service mines near Halifax—before Joan swiveled it back away from her.

"That is an incident from the late 1800s," she said, dissatisfaction and disapproval evident in her tone. "It might have been a personal vendetta, framing those two women, but neither of them are named in the article or the photograph, so I wouldn't be able to tell you anything about the family it happened to."

There was a moment of silence as Joan gazed at the screen again, looking at the picture. Dulci wasn't sure how she could be more specific. "But at least you believe me," she said in a tiny voice. Joan looked over at her abruptly.

"Of course!" She looked around the library, saw that the only people were over in the far corner in the children's section, and motioned for Dulci to sit down in front of the desk. "Let me tell you my family's story, Dulci. It's a strange one, but it could point to the reason why you're having visions about the past instead of the future."

Dulci's head cocked to the side at that. How would Joan's story tell her why she was seeing some other person's trials and travails?

Joan began in a low voice. "Many of the Indians had land stolen. Usually it was by wide government decree. Worse in the United States, believe me, but still pretty bad, still dishonest, out here. My family has a stranger story though, than that." She looked at Dulci's clear brown eyes, her own growing more intense.

"It was after the Acadians had been cast out, and the

Mi'kmaq had been told they could either leave with them or put down their arms against the British. They weren't out to conquer anything, they just wanted stay in their homes, so they did as the British said, farewelled their Acadian neighbors and family, and got on with life. With the crown's settlement, many new settlers came from England, and one of them befriended a daughter of the tribe, a girl named Kukuwi."

Dulci cocked her head again. *Where was this going?*

"Kukuwi learned English from this settler, a man from Scotland, whose wife had died. We don't know exactly what happened, but we do have a tiny snippet in the town newspaper from when the girl was killed, outside the cabin which this man had built for himself. He built it," Joan continued, with some added warmth, "after stealing the land it was on from the Mi'kmaq through some connection he had with a government official, that's pretty clear. But no one investigated, no one was brought to justice! The family she came from was angry of course, and the tribe threatened to storm the city hall, such as it was, but they were put down and forced to leave, and nothing was ever proven. Or at least nothing says the truth in the historical record. I believe she was murdered by that settler and lay there to bleed to death in the snow."

An image came to Dulci's mind of a girl her own age, at the edge of that knife swipe she'd seen last night. She shivered.

"Exactly. She was murdered, and it was covered up. That can't be forgiven. There's been a curse on our family ever since. I believe it is because the truth needs to be uncovered." Her eyes shone at Dulci, then she dropped her gaze, her voice lowering once again. "And I believe it is why Jesse suffers."

"Jesse?!" Dulci's surprised response caused the mother in the corner to look up at them. Joan's eyes darted over at the movement, then returned to Dulci. "Sorry," she whispered. Her mind whirled. Joan thought that something in the past was plaguing Jesse, that a past wrong, unrighted, had the power to cause some sort of Tourette's syndrome in her son. Joan believed that the Scottish settler was a killer and needed to be exposed, so that the curse would end. Dulci wasn't sure if she could go that far in her own belief. She sat looking at her hands, wondering how to respond.

"It's okay. Tuotu doesn't agree with me. But…that's why I spend so much time researching these historic grievances, because I think one of them may reveal the truth." Joan straightened up, clearing her throat. "And that you might be in a similar situation. So go carefully, Dulci." She smiled a faint smile, waiting for her to respond, expecting the interview to be over.

Dulci stood and nodded. "I will. I'll let you know if I see anything else." Her thoughts were still swirling around in her head like excited yapping dogs, and she couldn't put them in any order. Where could she be alone to think?

* * *

The *Provocation* was no longer in harbor. It had been sent south for some repairs and retrofits, her father had said. Dulci looked out from Slip #6, where she could see the mouth of the harbor opening up to the east, to what would become the Atlantic. The wind rustled, the gulls swooped, and she tried to sort through her thoughts and feelings, there in her perch by the government sheds.

The whole thing seemed to be getting bigger, more incredible. I mean, sure, having visions in itself was pretty incredible, but some people believed that it happened. So, she'd believe that. What else?

Was she seeing the past or the future? Or something that was neither, just a crazy symbol of something that might go wrong in her life? Dulci shook her head, denying that possibility until she was more desperate. She'd go with the past, since the Indian she'd seen had definitely been wearing the traditional costume of the Mi'kmaq tribe of the eastern Cape Breton coast.

That was another thing: was it something that happened *here*? Or was it something from half a world away, people that looked familiar to her, but that was just a trick, and it was really the Sioux or the Apache, or some other tribe native to the continent? No, she thought, feeling her gut instinct kick in. It was definitely *of this place.*

Then why was *she* seeing these visions? Why not someone in Joan's family? And why did the big Scotsman look so much like Finn? Dulci caught her breath. Finn's family. *Oh, God.* Finn's ancestor had been here in Cape Breton. *When?* He'd said when his family first came over from Scotland. When was that? It might not explain why she was the one this was happening to, but if Joan's story involved Finn's ancestor, his coming back to Glace Cove might have reignited that curse...

Dulci tossed her head abruptly. No, she didn't believe that. *Curses?* No.

But what other explanation was there?

And what was she supposed to do about it?

Chapter 10

*   *   *

Dulci's stomach was unsettled the whole night, after that hour sitting on the wharf, gazing out at the water as her thoughts drove her in circles. She'd hardly eaten at dinner, then had a big bowl of cereal and a pastry for breakfast, and her body was telling her that had been a mistake. She stood at the bottom of her driveway, waiting for the bus in the crisp morning air, staring out at the foggy horizon of water.

It was Tuesday. She hadn't done her homework for science or history, but hoped she could get it done on the bus or during the short break. She breathed deeply with her eyes closed, imagining that she was letting go of the tension in her body. *Everything is going to be okay. I told Joan, and she can do what she wants with the information. I'm done.* It was more hope than belief, but more than anything Dulci wanted to just get on with her second week of high school, this experience that was already so wild and thrilling and challenging. She liked Finn. She wanted to hang out with him again, with nothing but the usual nerves and fluttery feelings getting in their way. *Normal.*

The word brought a pang of bittersweet feeling with it, but there was the bus. Dulci climbed on, ignoring the feeling. No more visions. Done. Moving on.

She managed to get through her history questions during homeroom, and felt a little better about facing the day. *I can do this*, she thought. *I may have to drop out of the music group though*, she amended with a cringe as she saw the flyer hanging on the announcement board in her homeroom. The next group meeting was set for Friday, when the other kids Mr. McKenna had talked to would show up. Something twisted in her chest. She wanted to go, she wanted to meet those students who had a passion like hers. *Maybe*, she decided. *If it doesn't seem dangerous.*

At the break, she asked the French teacher if she could stay in the classroom to work on a project. For those twenty minutes she stayed hidden inside, finishing up her science reading and questions, while all the others made noise outside in the cold, bright sun. When the bell rang for fourth period, Dulci swallowed a little sigh and thanked Mrs. George, ducking into the hallway to get to math class.

When Mehron saw her in science, she gave her a strange look.

"What?" Dulci asked.

"Where have you been all day? I looked for you at break."

"Oh, I had to finish this," she said, whipping out the paper from her binder.

Mehron rolled her eyes, but Dulci felt an undercurrent of disappointment, disapproval. *Something.* They'd talk about it at lunch. For now, the evil science teacher was already collecting pages and talking about a quiz. They suffered through her pointed questions and finally reached the end of class. Dulci felt that some of what had been bothering Mehron had worn off, and she felt more at ease again. They went to sit at the far end of the cafeteria, bringing out their sandwiches and chatting about classes, crushes, the first game coming up for the girls' soccer team. Mehron was just asking her about the music club, and Dulci was edging around how to explain her feelings on the matter, when a tall shadow fell across their table.

"Oh, hey, Finn," Dulci said, a smile creeping across her face. She heard Mehron's unmistakeable ahem.

"Do you know Mehron? She's my best friend. We've gone to school together forever."

"Hi," Finn said.

"Hey," Mehron returned.

"What's up?" Dulci asked.

"I, um, well, I tried to find you at the break, but you weren't anywhere I could see."

"She was hiding in the girls' bathroom," Mehron broke in, eyes twinkling.

Dulci socked her one. "I was not. I was finishing up a homework assignment, so I stayed in my French classroom. Sorry. Looks like the whole world was looking for me this morning." She glared at Mehron.

"Oh. Well, I was just looking for you so I could ask you about a second date." Dulci's ears got really warm all of a sudden, and she tried to calm herself by looking at her hands on the table. She could see Mehron's barely-hid grin out of the corner of her eye.

"Oh. Um, sure. Yes?" She looked up at him. He had a look on his face that was somewhere in the middle of relaxed and eager and worried. Dulci smiled. "When?"

"How about Friday night? There's a music gig going on at the bar downtown. Well, in the party room of the bar, so we're allowed in," he amended with a grin.

"That sounds great! I wonder who it is playing…" Dulci knew most of the local groups.

"I can't remember— it was something with 'silver' in the name, though. I think they're from over in Margaree?"

"Huh, that's cool. I don't know anyone from out there." Dulci felt the skin on her back bristle in anticipation. This would be fun!

"Yeah, me neither." He gave them both a look that said he didn't know many people anywhere. "I'll come by to pick you up from your house if you like. We can get dinner at the bar, they told me their burgers are really good." Another surge through Dulci's system, this time deep in her stomach. A dinner date. This was, like, serious.

"Okay," she said, her voice a little less confident than she would have liked. Finn leaned over the table then, placing a hand on the edge nearest Dulci, and bringing his mouth close to her ear.

"Can't wait," he whispered. As he straightened, his other hand curled a piece of her hair around her ear. He flashed a lopsided smile at her, then at Mehron, who was watching in a stupor, and then turned and walked away. Dulci felt her body unfreeze slowly with the deep breath she took.

"Ho-Lee crap," Mehron said, as her eyes came back to focus on Dulci. "He must be seriously into you. That was… weird."

"Was not. Or if it was, it's just because I didn't know what to say."

"Well, I won't ague with that. I wouldn't have either. But…" Mehron looked in the direction Finn had left. "He just seems, I dunno, too experienced? Like maybe he thinks he's in a soap opera or something."

"Hey." Dulci was hurt. Her friend was popping the bubble she'd just felt like she was rising into the air with. "That's not nice."

"Well, sorry, but I'm just telling you what I think." Mehron sounded a little defensive. "It's nothing to do with Jesse, you know that, right?"

It was then that Jesse's warnings came back to her, as well as the possibility that Finn might be involved in some freaky vision-inducing, revenge-taking supernatural plot to make her go nuts. The bubble disappeared completely. A stomachache replaced it. She looked at her fig cookies and potato chips. They went back in her backpack.

"I know," Dulci replied, but the wind had gone out of

her sails. They didn't talk much during the rest of lunch, each thinking their own moody thoughts. When the bell rang, Dulci didn't feel the ordinary reluctance to suit up for P.E. At least she'd be moving around the field, not caught in her own web of recycled dreads and worries. She waved to Mehron and headed for the locker room.

They were doing their warm-up run around the field before starting a soccer scrimmage, Dulci somewhere in the middle of the spread-out pack. She was getting better at running, not breathing so unevenly after a full lap, and congratulating herself for this little improvement, when she happened to look to the ditch on her right.

It was a drainage ditch, filled up with leaves this time of year, and waiting to get cleared out before the snows started. Except there was snow already. An icy, blue-tinted swath of it carpeted the whole side of the path. Dulci stopped, and followed it back toward the school with her eyes, and her attention was caught by a lump in the snow a few yards off. She tried to walk toward it, but found her feet unable to move from the ground where she was. *No,* she thought. *Not another one.*

She shivered in the cold, wearing only her sweatpants and a t-shirt in a cold, starry night. She looked harder at the lump in the snow. The strange fog eventually thinned, and she tried to identify the trailing shapes as leathers or strips of wool. *No, that's—* and Dulci's mind froze. It was hair. Long, black hair. Like Mehron's. She gasped. It was a young girl, on her side, facing away from her, her hair swirling around her and her arm flung behind her in reckless abandon.

A terror gripped Dulci's insides; she cried out. She found her left foot moving, free, and stepped forward, pulling her right foot ever so urgently along with her. She rushed to where the girl lay, and saw in the moonlight that there was a dark stain on the snow, spreading from underneath the girl's middle. Dulci hesitantly touched the girl's shoulder to roll her over onto her back.

There it was: from her breastbone, down to her left side, a rending of the tough leather and soft wool that she'd worn. The dark stain on the snow was the blood that had pooled from the wound. Dulci's mind recoiled. She gazed at the girl's face, which held bits of fluffy snow, perched on her eyelashes, glinting in the powerful moonlight.

The girl couldn't have been more than ten years old. She looked like an ordinary Mi'kmaq girl: square-ish face, smooth brown skin, full lips, pronounced cheekbones and brow line. But she had that wool cape… it was a rough wool plaid, red and dark blue and black, perhaps cut down from a great kilt, Dulci thought.

What on earth was this, then? An Indian girl, a Scots coat, and a knife wound in the snow, but no knife. Dulci felt for a pulse in her throat, but there was none. She felt time stretch out and got lost in the inky blackness of the moonlit night.

This was a mystery, and a murder, and something supernatural she shouldn't fool around with. She looked around, her skin prickling again as she realized the entire place was the snow and the night and the girl; there was nowhere to go that looked like her high school field, where her classmates were dutifully pacing the track. Her heart started to pound in her chest as she tried to force down any thought of panic.

She heard a sound. A low moaning sort of sound: a keening. She scanned the horizon, looking for the source. Trees, nothing, nothing, trees. *What was that?* A shape was moving, left and right, growing larger. The keening was getting louder, rolling out in waves of disconsolate sobbing and intermittent cries of words Dulci couldn't make out. Her panic came back in triplicate. It was that man she'd seen—the one who looked like Finn. He was trudging through the snow, lurching this way and that, sobbing and crying out words angrily at no one. Maybe at his God.

What could she do? Her feet were no longer rooted to the ground, but where could she run? Pretty soon he would glance up and see her, and then she would be next. She imagined the knife in his hand, swiping out at her as it had at that other Indian man. She felt frozen to the spot with fear, unable to breathe, but aching to scream. The man looked up and stood still. She felt suddenly weak, like she wanted to just melt into the snow herself. She glanced down and caught sight of the girl's face again. The weakness fled, replaced by an anger so deep she let out a battle cry.

"Arrrggghhhhh!" she cried, tensing to run through the snow to get at the man who'd done this.

But once she stepped out into the snow drift, her next footfall landed on dry grass. She fell, so startled by the change was she. She stayed in that position, sitting on one hip and her other leg extended backward, her hands on the ground. She looked up at a dozen students in Glace Cove High sweatpants and t-shirts, standing in a semi-circle looking at her.

Oh my god, I am going to die, she thought. *How much did they see?*

One girl came over; her name was Candace. Dulci remembered joking with her during the safety video. "Are you okay, Dulci?"

"Yeah, I'm fine. Totally fine. I must have just tripped, that's all," Dulci rattled off, trying to appear normal.

"You let out a scream and a half there, we thought you'd seen a bear or something," Candace said, trying to make light of it, but still obviously worried about what had made Dulci act so weird.

"Oh, no, it was a snake. I'm terrified of snakes. Sorry if I scared anyone."

Snakes? There weren't snakes in Cape Breton, but who cares. *I have got to get home.* Coach Johnson had by now jogged over as well. "You okay, Dulci? You want to go see the nurse, if you're scraped up at all?"

"Um, sure. Good idea," Dulci agreed. *Good way to get me out of class, and maybe I can just go home. Home,* she thought, and it wasn't altogether a reassuring picture. Her parents would surely ask what had happened, and what could she tell them? A desperate fear began to tug at her again, and the sound of that keening from that man in the snow. She set off for the school building, trying to control her breathing.

They checked her out and could find nothing wrong, but assented when she said she wanted to go home. She called home and got her dad on the basement extension. Her voice was shaky as she asked him to come pick her up from school, and he came right away. His eyes roved her face, seeking an explanation, but he let her go to her room and climb straight into bed when they got home.

"Anything I can bring you, chérie?"

"Maybe some of Mom's herbal tea?"

"Coming right up."

"Thanks, Dad."

Dulci accepted the mug of tea a few minutes later and stayed hunched up against her pillows clutching it for several minutes. The warmth seeped from the mug into her hands through the blanket; it started to thaw her mind out too. *I may be going crazy,* she thought. *But no, possibly not, if what Joan says is true.* But then would she have to accept all of what Joan said? She shivered at the thought, spilling some of the tea on her blanket. She closed her eyes and let out a frustrated sigh. She went to get a wet washcloth and dab at the stain.

The image of the Indian girl was imprinted on her mind's eye. Hair flung out across the snow, curled up on her side, face smooth, spirit gone. Dulci opened her eyes again, wanting to shake it out of her head. Why? Why was she seeing these things? If it had already happened, what could she do? Just stand and watch and feel awful?

Joan had said that she was looking for the truth of what happened to her ancestor—a small girl… What if it *was* her? Dulci immediately felt like she would throw up. Closed her eyes again, focused on breathing, tried to shut out all racing thoughts. What if that girl she'd talked about—the name was something with a K—the one who'd learned English from the settler, what if that was the girl she'd seen, and the settler was the big Scot?

The pieces fell into place. The girl was wearing a coat remade from a large plaid. The man had been threatening another Indian, who'd been trying to protect her, maybe? But what was Dulci to do? Tell Joan what she'd seen? There was still no proof, unless Dulci wanted to go around town being the freaky girl who saw visions of the past, which wouldn't be solid proof, anyway. At least not for people like her parents. What could she do but watch?

But then she remembered: she'd moved this time. She'd touched the girl. The big man had seen her, or so she'd thought. *Oh holy*—a bodily fear seized Dulci then. If she could be spirited away like that, how would she ever be safe in her own time?

Chapter 11

* * *

She slept badly that night, and finally got out of bed at 5 AM, admitting defeat and getting out her homework. She got through her math assignment, her French passage, and her science reading before feeling hungry. She was feeling normal again, padding down the stairs to get some oatmeal, when the realization hit her again. *I'm not safe.*

She skittered to a halt in her socks, catching onto the doorjamb to the kitchen, looking furtively out the front window from the center of the house. Dark. That far north, this late in the autumn, this early in the morning, it was just *dark*. She saw some movement—the tree branches swaying—and heard the wind. She let out the breath she was holding, and flipped on the light. She walked slowly to the kitchen cabinet and poured herself oatmeal from a packet, added water, and stuck it in the microwave. Waited.

As she waited those sixty seconds, she wondered what had physically happened yesterday on the field. Had she disappeared? Could they still see her, walking over and touching something on the ground? Or had she gone to that other time briefly? She had moved the girl, so she supposed the man she saw could have touched her as well. If the other students had heard her scream and cry out, they must have looked over and she'd been *there*, right? Otherwise they would have totally freaked out. So, all she had to explain was why she'd gotten distracted, and then that she'd seen something in the ditch. That should work as a cover story. She hoped it would all just blow over. And that Finn wouldn't hear about it. *Finn.*

The microwave beeped and woke her out of her trance. Oatmeal and spoon in hand, she went back up to her room. One more assignment: reading for English Lit. It was a few passages from a medieval text, and even with all the annotations, Dulci found it required a lot of concentration. The Green Man, a legend of the old English forests.

By the time she'd finished both the reading and the oatmeal, it was time to catch the bus. She quickly washed her face and got dressed, gathering her things and some lunch items from the fridge before waving to her dad— *yes, I feel better*—and scooting out the door. There was a fine mist drizzling down now, and she pulled up her hood to keep it out. When the bus came, Mehron was on it, which was unusual, since she usually got a ride with her mother into town earlier in the morning. She was wearing a cute orange knit cap, her long hair flowing out from underneath, which made Dulci's stomach clench with the memory of long black hair in the snow. But she forced a smile, complimented the cap, and they settled into their seats next to each other.

Dulci felt a little of her fatigue lift as they rode along, but then when they separated, it all returned. Hardly any sleep made her feel sluggish and stupid. *But hey, at least I did my assignments*, she tried to cheer herself up. She went through classes in a kind of daze, the fear having moved over to make room for her fatigue. If any of the teachers noticed, they didn't remark on it.

When she got to P.E., she asked Coach Johnson if she might not sit on the sidelines today, since she was still feeling unwell since yesterday's crisis. He was either a softie or afraid of a lawsuit from her mother, because he let her sit on the bench while the others ran drills and held a scrimmage. Dulci sat in her coat, wishing she also had a blanket because she felt so cold. *Hey, at least it's not raining*, she told herself, but felt the power of her 'at least' statements waning from overuse.

The cold changed. Everything got foggy. Her senses prickling alert, Dulci turned to see a small figure approach from her left. When she emerged from Dulci's long shadow, she saw it was the Indian girl, wearing a leather dress which fell to her ankles, and the plaid which looped up over her head and then down to the ground. There was no knife wound, no grizzly blood trail behind her. The girl made eye contact with her, showing a pleasant interest.

Dulci glanced back to her right: no field, no orange cones, no coach yelling corrections. She was still seated, but it was on a tree stump. And the field had turned into a grassy hill, bathed in golden morning sun. The ground rolled up to the top, where there were a few small trees and a small structure. Behind her sat the shoreline and the sea beyond. Dulci looked back up the hill and saw smoke coming out of a little chimney.

"Hel-o," the girl said, startling Dulci out of her perusal of the land.

"Hello," she replied, her attention back on the girl.

"What your name?" she asked Dulci.

"Dulci," she replied.

The girl's smile got slightly wider. "My name Kukuwi. Where your come from?" She said the words with careful attention.

"I come from Glace Cove," Dulci answered, wondering how that would be received. Was it even called that yet, whenever these people lived?

Kukuwi nodded once, making no comment. Her eyes traveled over Dulci's black Levi's, her flannel shirt and hoodie and bright blue winter coat.

"You're a spirit," she said. "Welcome. Who your come for help?" Her eyes were curious.

"I think I've come to help—you," Dulci answered truthfully. Kukuwi's eyes widened for a second, then she nodded.

"That mean your help for Angus too. Please help for land and my family. They need understanding."

A shout went up from the top of the hill. Kukuwi turned to look. A figure waved its arm once, and she answered with a big wave. She turned to Dulci, who was squinting to see who was waving at the top. All she could see was some light hair and a great grey blanket. A great kilt. It was—

"Thank you. Please help for my tribe. They need understanding." And she was off, trotting up the hill.

Dulci reached forward to set off after her—*No, you can't go to him, he's going to kill you, he threatened one of your tribe!*—when the hill vanished and she was once again on the field, outlined in white spray paint, covered with orange cones for the soccer drills. She glanced around. No one was looking at her, they were all weaving in and out of the cones, aiming shots for the goalie down at the far edge of the field.

At least I didn't scream this time, Dulci thought. But she immediately became aware that she was going to be sick. She crept over behind the bench she'd been sitting on, and threw up. She tried to be as quiet as she could, but the coach was back over by her side in a minute.

"You need to go home again, Dulci? Poor thing. I hope it's not the first of the flu," he was saying. He blew his whistle and all the other students ran in towards the center line.

"We're finishing up ten minutes early today. Could someone volunteer to help Dulci to the nurse's office? Be careful; go slow."

Candace volunteered and they walked slowly back up

to the main building. She didn't ask any questions, but Dulci could sense her intense curiosity being reined in. After the nurse checked her out and gave her an antiemetic for her stomach, she called her dad again. When he arrived, Dulci had come to a decision.

"Can you take me to the Tebneks'? I think I need to talk to Jesse."

Chapter 12

* * *

"Jesse? Jesse Tebnck? But why?" Her father's expression was bewildered, not expecting such an answer. "I thought he was…" He searched for a kind word.

"He is. He has some kind of mental problem. But I want to know if he's been having visions like I have."

"Visions? What are you talking about, Dulci?"

"I tried to tell you about the first one, but you wouldn't listen. I've had two more—three more! And they keep getting weirder! Just drive down to the Mi'kmaq harbor village. I need to ask him."

"Dulci," here her father gave her a pitying look. "I'm sorry if I didn't listen. If you're having troubles, I will listen. I thought it was something about the boy who asked you out."

"It is! Let's just go, Dad. I can tell you more later, if I know any more after we go talk to Jesse or Joan."

"Okay," he said doubtfully, but pulled away from the curb.

* * *

When they got to the Tebneks' single-story house, Dulci dashed out and ran to knock on the door. Everything felt so *urgent*.

Moments feeling like hours, as she waited for someone to answer. It was only three o'clock, so Mehron wouldn't be home yet. Would Joan?

Finally, the door was pulled open: Joan. Her dad stood behind her now, and started to speak. "Hi, Joan. Sorry to—"

"Joan, I had another one. Two. I need to talk to Jesse. He's here, right?"

Joan looked from Don to Dulci as they spoke. After a slight hesitation, she nodded and stepped back for them to enter.

"He's in his room. Be careful."

Dulci paced the hallway and came to the door before the kitchen. She heard her father start in on Joan. *You knew about this, Joan?* But Dulci blocked out the voices. She knocked lightly on Jesse's door, but received no response. Knowing that she was entering the domain of a teenage boy, she opened the door slowly, half-afraid of what she might see. Jesse was there, all right, kneeling alongside his bed, rocking back and forth with his hands crunched up under his eyes. He wore his typical all-black ensemble of jeans, t-shirt, and hoodie. He didn't look up.

"Hey, Jesse?" He stopped his rocking back and forth. "It's Dulci."

He buried his head even further down, raking his hands upward through his tangled hair. With what looked like an extreme effort, he rocked back slowly on his heels and looked around at her. His face was streaked with tears, his eyes bleak. Dulci stepped back half a pace.

He waited for her to speak for a moment. What to say to that face? She'd known him when he was younger, when he had teased his sister and her friend, laughing and joking with them. He'd been a fun older brother then. What was he experiencing, keeping at bay, that was creating all that pain?

"I want to talk to you—about Kukuwi."

Jesse's eyes stayed fixed on her, but she saw the rise and fall of his chest pick up speed. He put out a hand toward the bed and pulled himself up, still going slowly. He sat on the bed, finally breaking eye contact with her to drop his gaze to the floor.

"What is there to say? If you've seen her, you know." He said the words softly, but despite their defeatist tone, Dulci saw the muscles in his neck flex hard against the statement.

"Am I the first person to see her, besides you?"

"Mm-hmm."

"What did you see?"

"I saw her dead in the snow with a knife wound, and the knife laying close by. I see a big angry Scottish bastard swinging the knife around too, looking like he wanted to kill me." His eyes found hers again. "But I want to kill *him*. Because I've seen Kukuwi's brother Taytere also, and he vows revenge." He canted his head slightly. "Have you seen Taytere? He kind of looks like me. Or I look like him," he added with a smile that didn't reach his eyes.

Dulci was shaking her head, but then thought of the Indian man that the Scot had been threatening with his knife. Was that Taytere? She'd only seen him from the back, but it could have been. She looked at Jesse again, and his eyes softened; he'd seen her remembering. He stood up and crossed his arms, letting her look at him.

He stood at almost the height of her dad, who was just shy of six feet. He had straight black hair like his sister, but he'd done something to it to make it spiky. Besides being tangled, he might have ratted it to make it stand up. His features and limbs were long and graceful, but they were marred by the terrible pain with made him stand so rigidly, and hold his face with such control. His crossed arms showed her a broad chest, and wider shoulders than most boys she knew at that age. Yes, he could have been that shorter man.

"Maybe I only saw his back."

Jesse's shoulders seemed to relax a fraction more, and his brows contracted slightly. "So. Now you'll go crazy with it too." He sat back down on the bed gingerly. "Have you told anyone else?"

"I tried to tell my dad, but he doesn't believe in it. I told your mom."

"Not Mehron?"

"No." Dulci twinged guiltily when she said this. She wanted to, but something still held her back, something told her she wouldn't believe any of it either. And then she'd have a crazy brother to deal with *and* a crazy friend on her hands. "Did you tell Mehron?"

"No, not for a while. I tried at the beginning, four years ago, but it just got too—hard." Dulci saw the gulp, the pain of losing your sister slowly and by degrees. She didn't want it to happen to her. She was desperate to find out why it was happening and what they could do to stop it. But her only other witness was here telling her he'd learned nothing in four years. *Four years.* Dulci's heart seemed to drop like a stone as she registered that reality. She swallowed with difficulty. A sound from the living room reached her and she made a movement to turn, but stopped.

"Do you know what happened? Do you know why we're seeing this—this stuff?" She spoke softly so her voice wouldn't carry back to the other parts of the house.

"I saw Taytere, and he called for revenge. I see him now, all the time. I figure he wants me to find that Scotsman's family and—hurt them." As he said it, Jesse's shoulders rolled in defensively.

"Revenge for what? And would—would you do it?"

"Revenge for killing his sister. He killed Kukuwi with the knife and then cursed our family. I—*I would*—dammit!" He placed his face in his hands, propping his elbows on his knees, his feet on the bedrail. "I think I have to, to make it stop. I don't want to actually do it, but what else am I supposed to do?" He raked his hair back again, staring at Dulci with haunted eyes. Obviously he'd wrestled with this question before.

"And that's what your mom thinks too?"

His gaze switched to the opposite wall. "Maybe. She believes I see things, but isn't sure why, what I'm supposed to do about it." Pretty much what she'd told Dulci.

"Well, what do you think I'm supposed to do with it? Why me?"

The question seemed to catch him by surprise. His head turned toward her, and the alarm on his face frightened her. "I don't know. Your family's mostly Acadians, right?" She nodded, but he was already continuing. "So you're not *that* family. Only—" He looked at her, his stare getting more intense. "You said something about a MacDonald boy, no?"

Ohmigod, Finn. How had she forgotten? He played a part in all this too. He was in the visions. Or that guy who looked like him. And he had that story about the ancestor who'd had bad luck around Glace Cove and so wandered the plains of Canada, turning into a ghost. *A ghost.*

Dulci's breath came out in a sharp gasp. She stepped back and felt the wall behind her. A second later, Joan was at the doorway. She took in Jesse sitting on the bed and Dulci leaning on the wall. "Everything OK?"

Dulci couldn't look her in the eye, or the terror would be obvious. She nodded, closing her mouth. Jesse said something to her she didn't hear. Joan seemed satisfied though, and went back to the living room to continue talking with Don.

"Finn MacDonald. He's new at school. His family just moved back to the Cove after a long time." She took a shuddering breath, remembering Jesse's last Frankenstein-like speech about staying away from Finn. "He looks like the Scotsman in the visions."

Jesse leapt to his feet, exulting momentarily in the middle of the small room, a comic book super-villain. "I knew it!" But then he crumpled right back, this time settling on the floor in front of the bed, drawing his knees up to his chest and holding them tight. "So what do

I do… Taytere—he got worse right before school started. More angry. I didn't know why. Now I guess we do."

Dulci strained to keep a hold on her composure. Painful tears stood in her eyes, making Jesse a blurry form now on the floor. "He doesn't know about any of this, Jesse. And he's innocent. He's—he's a nice guy. You can't—can't hurt him." She hiccuped on the last bit, the tears finally streaking down her cheeks. She saw Jesse looking at her oddly. "We're friends. You can't hurt him. Besides, what would happen to you?" Her voice got a little stronger.

A harsh exhalation was all the reply Jesse made to that. "Doesn't seem to matter, does it?" He looked away again.

Dulci felt her heart being torn in two directions. She went to Jesse, sitting in front of him cross-legged, and put her hand on his shoulder. He didn't look up. "Yes, it does. It matters to me and Mehron, and your mom and dad. And lots of other people too. You can't do it." She squeezed his shoulder for emphasis. "We'll figure it out. We've got two heads working on it now, plus your mom. That's better, right?" That fleeting smile passed over his face again. He touched her elbow briefly, then folded his arms across his legs again and put down his head.

Well, thought Dulci, *at least I'm not crazy alone anymore.*

Chapter 13

* * *

Don hadn't grilled her on the ride home, but when Olive came home for dinner, he started a discussion at the dinner table. Dulci didn't feel like eating, but tried to act normal and appreciate the apple tart that was one of her favorites.

"Honey, I think we need to discuss some problems Dulci's been having at school."

"Already?" Olive asked, her head swiveling to the right to look at Dulci. "What happened?"

"It's not just at school," Dulci mumbled.

"What's that? I didn't hear you," said Olive.

"It's not just at school. One of them happened at home, too," she said loudly.

"One of what?" Olive looked at Don, but he waited with an expectant expression.

"You guys aren't going to believe me anyway," Dulci said.

"But we are going to listen to what you have to say, Dulci," her dad said. Guess she couldn't get out of it.

"I've had three—no, four—visions since school started. I thought at first I had the Second Sight," this earned her a frown from her mom. "But then I realized I was seeing scenes that happened in the past. Here. In Glace

Cove. At least I think I am. And Jesse Tebnek has seen some of the same things." A thick silence greeted this last statement.

"The scenes we've seen involve a big Scottish man, and a little Mi'kmaq girl, and her brother. Probably," she added. She wanted to be as accurate as possible, and she wasn't certain that she had seen Taytere. Not like they were going to believe this anyway. She continued, making it as short as possible.

"The Scottish guy was waving a knife around and acting pissed off, but at different times, and then later—later, we saw the girl dead of a knife wound."

Another thick silence hung in the dining room. Dulci's apple tart seemed to congeal and discolor in front of her eyes. No way she could finish it now. "The girl's name is Kukuwi, and she talked to me a little bit. But we're still trying to figure out why we're seeing these scenes. Jesse thinks it has to do with a curse on his family, started by the MacDonalds. They *may* be related to the Scottish guy in the vision." She didn't tell them it had to be so, because he looked like he could've been Finn's father. No need to disclose more than necessary detail.

Her hand held her fork lightly, resting on the table. She was looking down at her plate, waiting for some reaction. It finally came from her mother. "Have you been watching scary movies? This has got to be your imagination, Dulci, and the Tebnek boy is just pulling your leg. Either that or—"

"Or what, Mom?" Dulci looked up at her, stung by the dismissal even though she'd expected it.

"Or you're getting into trouble I've never even dreamed of! I didn't think drugs were a problem at the high school, but if I find that you've been smoking something—"

"Honey," Don reached for Olive's hand. His voice stilled and soothed. "I don't think either of us believe that you're getting into drugs, Dulci. We know you're a good kid, and a good daughter. We're just worried about what's happening since it seems to be affecting your health and your ability to attend school. That's two days in a row I've had to pick you up early." Olive's eyebrows shot upward at this; apparently he hadn't told her yet.

"Is there something you can sit out on, that might bring the stress level down? I know starting a new school and all can be stressful."

Dulci was miserable. Her mom didn't believe her; her dad was already treating her like a mental patient. What could she say?

She shook her head. "I'm not really doing anything, Dad. Just the music club, but it hasn't even started yet."

"But isn't that when you said the first vision happened?"

"Yeah, but—"

"Then I think maybe that's where we have to start. I'll have a talk with this Mr. McKenna."

Misery took on a new hue. She wasn't even going to be allowed to be in the music club she'd helped to start. Could this get any worse?

"And I don't want you going near that Tebnek boy again," put in Olive. "He's obviously a corrupting influence. Mehron can come here, or you can hang out in town, but not at their house. Is that understood?"

Dulci swallowed. She nodded. "Can I go up to my room now?"

"You don't want the rest of your apple tart?" She shook her head, trying not to let the nausea show.

"Okay, then. Try to get a good night's rest; that should help."

"Good night, Dulci," said her dad. She didn't meet their eyes as she trudged up the stairs. No music. No Tebneks. But the visions would keep coming. She could feel it.

* * *

Don let Dulci stay home the next day, calling into the

school to assure them she was under the weather, not playing hooky. Dulci sat on her bed late in the morning, hugging one of her old stuffed animals to her chest. She figured she'd stay in her pajamas the whole day, just because. She'd arranged with Finn to go to that bar the next evening, and didn't feel like texting him about the developments at home, even though she had his number now. Again, what could she say?

"Hey, Finn, your ancestor did this terrible thing, so now my best friend's brother thinks he needs to kill you. Maybe you'd better leave town?"

Yeah. Not going to work. She did some of her homework to get her mind off her impossible situation, and fell asleep a couple times. By early afternoon she was feeling a little better just from the rest. She went downstairs and saw her mom had left a note about some beef broth in the fridge she could heat up. That sounded good.

She heard her phone get a text from several rooms away, and went to answer it. It was Finn.

Hey, heard u r sick. That real? Hope u feel better. Let me know if u feel OK to go out to the ceilidh tmw nite

Dulci stared at the little lit-up screen. What if she asked Finn about whether he'd felt funny since coming back to Glace Cove? Maybe he'd had something *like* a vision. But he sure hadn't seemed bothered by anything, and they seemed to bother both Jesse and her a lot. *No, he probably hasn't seen anything after all.* And what could he do, to make anything better? Nothing. Dulci set her phone back on the kitchen counter. *Nothing.*

The screen flashed at her again. From Mehron:

"Mom said you visited last night, bf I got home. Now you're out sick. What's up?"

The nausea from last night came back. She couldn't go to their house anymore, which meant she likely wouldn't get to talk to Jesse, since he was basically housebound. She would have to tell Mehron everything. She texted back to Mehron.

Can u come over after school? Need 2 talk.

She got an answering emoticon and clicked off the phone.

She poured out some of the beef broth her mom had defrosted and popped it in the microwave. Grabbed a slice of the large wholegrain bread on the counter. Made a cup of tea with water from the kettle. Then took three trips carefully up the stairs again to sit with her meal in her room. She tried to be careful about crumbs, but felt sleep tugging at her eyes and fingertips as soon as she sipped the last spoonful. *Ahhhh*, her body wanted to relax.

Dulci woke abruptly when it was already midnight blue outside her window. She looked at the clock on her wall: only half past seven. Had she missed Mehron then? When she thundered down the stairs, she learned from her mother that she had: Mehron had been by, but Olive had looked in at Dulci sleeping and asked her to come back the next day.

"Gah!" Dulci exhaled in frustration. It would have to wait.

Even normally, Dulci detested waiting. She went back up to her room and tried to tackle another homework assignment. History again, this time an article on the migratory history of peoples in Nova Scotia. It was interesting because it was from the point of view of an Acadian-descended scholar. His family had been one of the early French settlers cast out after trouble with subsequent British rule. The author compared both the British movements, low-born and high-born, and the Aboriginal patterns of hunting and gathering, which were replaced by containment on government Reserves.

It was a dazzling scope of history to try to fit in one article, and Dulci found herself at a loss as to how she was going to summarize it even more into a paragraph for her midterm notes. Her thoughts drifted between the European settlers and the original M'ikmaq. She dreamed of a dance with all three groups: British, Mi'kmaw, and

Acadian. They were dancing across a map of Cape Breton Island, dipping toes into the ocean and swinging from its high peaks.

Chapter 14

* * *

Dulci was determined to go to school the next day, armed with the best reason of all against her parents: 'I don't want to fall behind!'

It worked. Olive and Don agreed she should go back to school, but not yet to the Tebneks'. Her father would talk with the school nurse about the incidents she'd observed when he dropped her off. Dulci accepted the conditions, thinking it didn't really matter: what would happen would happen.

She scraped through her classes, explaining her absence with a stomach bug and not volunteering once in any of her classes. She saw Mehron at the break, but gave her the same explanation and stayed passive, listening to her friend chatter about what she'd missed but biding her time until she could tell her the whole story.

After the missed opportunity last night, she was afraid again. She didn't want to tell Mehron and have to face her skepticism. She'd told three people so far: two had believed, one had not. If Mehron didn't, Dulci might have to reconsider whether she was going nuts. She hadn't asked for this new role; she didn't see why she had to right this wrong that she hadn't committed. *If anyone, it should be Finn doing it*, she thought. *If it is actually his family,* she amended. Her mind wandered back to the girl who had addressed her as a spirit just as the teacher called on her for an answer. She blinked and tried to remember what she'd half-heard a moment ago, but there was no chance. Neither disapproval nor pity was on the teacher's face, however, when it swept across the room to transfer the question to another student. Maybe they'd all been told she was a freak. Maybe they were all under orders to humor her. *Okay, stop the paranoia thoughts right now*, Dulci told herself.

She sat through P.E again. When the bell rang, she was more than usually eager to leave the field bench. The coach had been periodically checking on her while he ran the other students through drills, as if he thought she might disappear herself. It annoyed Dulci to be thought so unreliable. Then again, maybe she had disappeared for a moment. Also, she felt the chill of the corner of the field where she'd seen Kukuwi. It was like a glacier sat there, and she could feel its cold tendrils of air sweeping across toward her. She succeeded in not looking that direction for the full fifty minutes: the day was a success. Now, if only she could get through this dinner date with Finn.

* * *

She went home to do some homework and change. Her parents didn't do too much hovering, but when one considered how long of a lead they usually gave her, the few pointed questions they did ask seemed suffocating. At least she hadn't met with resistance when she told them about the date tonight. They might have said no because it had to do with music, but she surmised they acquiesced because it was with Finn, the fine upstanding young man they were glad she was interested in. *Hmmph*, Dulci thought about that. *If they knew what his ancestor had done, they wouldn't let me go out on the town with him, I bet.*

She was all ready at five o'clock, dressed in a dark denim pair of trousers and a soft green turtleneck. In lieu of a bosom, that would have to do. She put on lip balm and a ribbon headband, and then pondered the possible outcomes of the night.

Option #1: the food is good, we talk about normal stuff, the music is great, and the date is a success

Outlook: Not likely.

Option #2: the food is good, I ask Finn about why his ancestor might have murdered a little girl in cold blood a couple hundred years ago, he ditches me, the music is still good, but I die of embarrassment because I have to call my dad to pick me up.

Outlook: Entirely possible.

The doorbell rang, and she tried to squelch the thrills of fear in her gut. *Just treat it as a fun night with a friend, and see if there's an opening for asking about that old MacDonald.* The flutters calmed down a fraction. She grabbed her small canvas messenger bag for her phone and camera and wallet and yelled goodbye to the house before stepping out and closing the front door behind her.

"Hi," she said to a surprised Finn, who had scooted back a step to make room for her sudden appearance. *He must've thought I'd invite him in, like a normal person. Oh well. Too late for that.*

"Hey," came the reply. "You ready to go?"

"Yep." Dulci put on her as-real-as-possible-under-the-circumstances smile, and walked with him out to the old green pick-up. It didn't have power locks, so once again he took the trouble to open her side first and let her in. Once she'd climbed in, he shut the door and paced around the front. When he got in the driver's seat, she was just finishing wrestling with her cranky seatbelt when he leaned over and kissed her on the cheek. Surprised, she looked up at him.

His face broke into a wide smile.

"What—what was that?" she said.

"That—was—nice," he said, punctuating each word with a pause. "I'm sorry, but your expression—" He broke into a guffaw and looked away.

Dulci frowned and faced forward. Was he making fun of her?

"Dulci, you just looked so shocked. I've been wanting to kiss you since the first day of school. I just didn't think you'd look so—like you'd seen a ghost!" He laughed, and while Dulci could relax about his making fun, his choice of words couldn't have done more to put her further on edge. Just treat it as a fun night? That was going to be rough; Fate seemed to be working against her.

* * *

A server seated them at a table and they ordered: Finn got the hamburger and Dulci, after some waffling, got the fish and chips. Pub grub. She'd been here once before, but it was long ago; she barely remembered. If she'd known they had regular ceilidh nights, she'd have been back sooner.

They talked about school, about plans, about sports, the same stuff kids her age usually did. Dulci had already dismissed the kiss in the truck, since it hadn't produced any of the feelings in her that she thought a kiss would. She was now focused on the task of telling Finn about the visions and their relation to his family. She hoped he wouldn't freak out so that she'd have to call her dad.

A lull descended as the food arrived, steaming and fragrant. *Better plunge in then*, Dulci thought.

"So, I was thinking about that ancestor you had that you said had the Sight?" It tumbled out in a mumbly heap.

"That ancestor that what? Oh yeah, the ghost. What about him? Have you seen any more visions?"

"Yes." She said it in a studied, quiet voice, and that made Finn raise his eyebrows. "I saw someone who looks like you, I told you that." Finn nodded. "I've also seen him waving a knife at a young Mi'kmaq man. And then, on the field at school, I saw a little Mi'kmaq girl dead from a knife wound." She let out a big breath. Would he get defensive right away? Would he know what had happened?

When she looked up at him, he looked back at her with a small frown of confusion. "So what has that got to do with my ancestor?"

"It's someone from your family, Finn, I know it."

"Can you tell when he's from? Any sort of name or date?"

"No, it's always in the snow, so the people are covered in clothing, coats and furs, but I know it's olden times."

"Olden times… but that could be the eighteenth century or the twentieth, Dulci!"

"But I know someone has seen the same things, and he knows when they happen!"

"Who?" came Finn's sharp reply.

"Mehron's brother. Jesse Tebnek." Dulci looked down as she said it, feeling like she was putting Jesse in danger somehow.

A look of comprehension crossed Finn's face. He put down the hamburger he'd only taken a few bites from. "Are you going out with him? I thought he was some kind of mental case."

"He's not—" Dulci modulated her voice from the screech she'd started with to a low dignified murmur. "He's not a 'mental case.' He's been seeing similar visions to mine for longer, that's all, and he doesn't know what to do about it any more than I do." Dulci looked at her chips. "He used to be a really nice, normal, older brother."

"Uh-huh." Finn's gaze appraised her coolly, and she didn't like it one bit. "What?"

"Oh, nothing. I just thought you'd be more *available*, that's all. Not always babbling about some weird delusions or your history with some other guy I don't know."

Dulci was so shocked she gaped at him for a moment. "I wanted to tell you because it is something between your family and his, and there has been wrong done, *wrong!*" She balled her fist and banged the table to emphasize the word further.

"And what do you expect me to do about it?" he asked. He dismissed the whole issue with his next glance toward the band.

Dulci turned away, mortified.

"Dulci, I like you, but I can only handle so much *weird.*"

Her mortification became a migraine deep in her skull. She felt her throat close up with tears.

"How about we don't talk any more about visions and family history tonight? Let's just enjoy the music." The musicians were adjusting their seats and tuning their instruments.

Dulci sniffled loudly, half-nodded, and then grabbed her small bag before heading over to the ladies' room. Once safely in its white confines, she stood alone in front of the mirror. She set her bag down, relaxing her fingers that felt like talons.

Should have known it was too good to be true.

Should have known he couldn't really be interested in me.

Should have known being myself would turn him off at some point.

The hateful thoughts swirled in her head, and she had a hard time turning them off. She splashed some cold water on her hands and placed them on the back of her neck, then the inside of her elbow. She felt her skin cool, and her mind pay attention.

I'm going back out there and I'm going to be normal. I'm going to enjoy the jam session but not worry about Finn, or the visions, or anything. Just be in the moment.

Another few repetitions and she stood a little taller. She marched out of the ladies' to see Finn conversing with the waitress briefly. His eyes sparkled and the smile lit up his face. When she left, his expression calmed to almost-vacant, practically asleep. *Enjoy the music. Be in the moment.*

She managed to get through the set that lasted until nine. She felt hardness and frustration ease out of her chest while she listened and clapped along, but the ice and uneasiness crept back in whenever she glanced over at Finn. He looked like he'd had a good time when he dropped her off, but didn't lean in for a kiss at the door, as she'd been afraid he might. Instead, Dulci was left to ponder a night of mixed signals and undisguised disdain as she drifted off to sleep.

Chapter 15

* * *

The next day dragged slowly by, with no improvement in Dulci's ability to focus on her homework. She read through the Thomas Hardy excerpts, pondering Finn's perspective as she tried to find evidence of the Wheel of Fate. She did her science equation problems while trying to pinpoint the time period when the visions might have occurred. By afternoon, her mind and body were both spent.

Mehron could even sense was something wrong via text: her gentle teasing about Finn had yielded nothing, so she backed off and left Dulci to her sulk. Dulci was sitting in the armchair on the back porch when she thought about another source of help: the library, and Joan. She hurried to dress for outside and headed out in the direction of town. She tried to jog, but her large backpack made an ungainly galumphing rhythm to her walk, so she settled for walking quickly.

Fifteen minutes later, she was in the library. She didn't know if Saturday was one of Joan's days volunteering, but she crossed her fingers: yes, there she was, behind the desk. This time, however, she wasn't staring at the computer screen, but talking to an adult standing in front of her. She decided to wait on the other side of the room.

But as soon as she heard the adult's voice, she froze mid-step and turned to look back. It was her mother, Olive, dressed impeccably as always, with the addition of a grey trench coat. She was leaning over Joan's desk in an intimidating manner, one hand on its surface. Dulci crept back toward them, staying behind two layers of shelves.

"Well, all right. If Mehron hasn't shown any signs of this craziness, she's welcome to come visit at the house, but I don't want Dulci near Jesse anymore. We can't have some Blair Witch-type madness starting up here in our little town. We can't encourage them. We'll do what we can to keep in touch with Dulci and make sure she doesn't have any added stressors. I hope you'll do the same for your family."

To this speech of Olive's, Joan stoically looked forward and down, at about the level of Olive's belt. She nodded slightly.

"Okay then, thanks, Joan. Let's not let this get out of hand. Good luck with your—good luck." Olive turned past Dulci's hiding spot, and headed out the door. Dulci stared after her, only realizing after a couple minutes that she was breathing loudly, probably being heard by anyone around. She gulped and closed her mouth, looking back to where Joan sat. She was still staring at the same place, unmoving.

Dulci peeked out from the rows. "Joan?"

Joan turned her head slowly to her voice. When she saw who it was, she closed her eyes and tilted her head upward. A short sigh blew from between her lips, choked off abruptly. "Dulci, did you overhear that?"

She came completely out of the stacks and stood next to the desk. She nodded.

"What do you think?"

"About what? About what she said? Or about the whole situation?"

"About what she said."

"I disagree. I don't have any big stresses that would

cause this. It's like I told you before, they're visions!" She rasped it out *sotto voce*, still aware that there might be others in the small library. "She and Dad don't believe me. And even—even Finn doesn't believe me. You're my only hope, Joan. I don't know how to live with this, and I don't know how to solve it either. I just want it to *stop*."

Joan didn't reply for some moments. She sat contemplating the papers on her desk, struggling with some emotion. Finally, she met Dulci's eyes. "Why is it you? Do you know yet?"

"Because I'm the link between the two families. We figured that out."

"Who's 'we' then?" Joan asked.

"Jesse and me. Mom and Dad are angry because they think he's passing on the crazy to me. But it's not him, it's Kukuwi—I think she's trying to reach us both—"

"Who's that? Kukuwi."

"She's the Mi'kmaq girl. I've seen her. Jesse's seen her." Dulci swallowed painfully past a sudden lump. "We both saw her dead. But I talked to her, too, which Jesse hadn't done. But Jesse talked to Taytere, which I haven't done…"

"Taytere… Kukuwi…" Joan began shuffling through some of the layers on her desk again. Slowly, she moved the plastic sleeves with the photocopies of old fragments of text, looking for one in particular.

Dulci watched her shuffle, and spoke softly. "She talked to me. Assumed I was a spirit. Sent to help. Meant to help Angus as well as herself. Is one of your stories about an Angus? He must be the one that killed her." Saying it made her mouth go dry. "Maybe she can't appear to Finn. Otherwise, I don't know why—" but Joan had found what she was looking for: a newspaper fragment from the village of Baddeck in the year 1777. It showed a political cartoon about the American colonies, and below that, there was a small announcement:

"In order to Resolve a most dangerous Unrest, a partial band of the Mick Mack Indian settlement has been moved South West at the behest of Town Fathers charged with the Protection and Security of Glace Cove.

Being that an Allegation of One of the Families, a Claim that some parcel of their tribal property was stolen by one Mr. Angus Mac-Donald, recent member of the Colony, was found to be spurious, and being that the family in question has continued to threaten Riot and uncivil Discourse in regards to matters of the Crown's Treaty, the sitting Judge at Baddeck, the Right Honourable C. H. MacGillicuddy, finds that only their speedy removal will resolve the Matter in accord with the Peace and Security of the People of Glace Cove.

In a related Matter, a young Mick Mack girl was found dead under mysterious and violent Circumstance. The body of the Victim was found near the temporary dwelling of said A. MacDonald, but it is unknown how she came to be there.

His Honour has allowed Mr. MacDonald to remain in the dwelling on his land."

Joan's voice floated over them both. Who knew what she was imagining, but Dulci was seeing the Scotsman again, drunkenly weaving and crying out, brandishing the long, ugly knife in the moonlight. Now he had a name: Angus MacDonald. And a time: 1777. Something clicked into place.

"When Kukuwi said to help Angus, maybe she meant that she knew what he would do, and she wanted me to prevent his—doing it," she said, unwilling to speak the deed aloud again.

"That is possible," Joan allowed. "But I thought she would—I'm sorry," she ducked her head and covered her mouth with her hand. "I thought if there were a further sign, it would be something to help Jesse. He's been suffering for four *years*. Not that bloody *Angus*." Already the name in the article had been transformed into the basket for all her held-in hate. Dulci could see the despair in her, waiting to jump out at something, someone tangible, a simple name.

"Joan?" With an effort, Joan drew herself back in, sitting up straighter in her seat. Dulci reached across the desk to grab her hand before she became too reserved again. "I don't know what I'm supposed to do, but if I see some way to prevent Kukuwi's death, I'll do it. I don't care about Angus. I care about you guys: my friends." She got an answering squeeze of her hand before it was withdrawn.

"You're a good girl, Dulci. Thank you." She stopped, puzzled. "But you haven't told Mehron any of this. Is there a reason why?"

Dulci cleared her throat and scrunched up her shoulders briefly. "I was going to, day before yesterday, but I was asleep when she came by. I meant to," she repeated with confirmation. But school doesn't seem the place for it. Would you tell her? Would she believe it—us?"

An answering resigned gleam in her eyes told Dulci that Joan felt the same. Mehron would probably deny the Sight, as Tuotu had been trying to do. "I don't know, but I'll tell her all the same."

"Thanks." Dulci felt a weight lifted, at the same time as she straightened and saw the clock on the wall behind Joan. "I'd better get home before I'm missed," she said. "Thank you, Joan. I'll let you know if—if anything else happens."

Chapter 16

* * *

She lay on her bed, her hands behind her head, her legs crossed at the ankle, on top of the comforter. Thoughts were swirling through again, trailing behind them the new emotions she had to decide what to do with. She'd hidden from her mother in the library and talked to Joan expressly against her wishes. It felt wrong, and out of sync with the good girl image she had of herself, but the icky feeling wasn't enough to make her stop. She had to know.

She'd come home early enough so that there was no comment about it. Her dad had asked her about her walk. Her mom had asked her about math class. She'd made up some answers, but didn't bother to hide her depressed spirits. It was a quiet dinner.

She sat on the bed, contemplating this new complication. She didn't mean to rebel, but they didn't believe her, despite all the good she'd done. Her spotless record mattered for nothing, it seemed. She'd done some of her reading and science problems but still had a history essay to start. Maybe she could manage an outline at least, in this droopy state.

Questions: Pick One.

Which of the early explorers best illustrated the characteristics of the Age of Exploration? Support your answer.

Which of the peoples of the new lands 'discovered' by the Europeans in the 15th century fared the best, and which the worst?

The questions seemed to make no sense. Either that, or she was so bored by them her brain refused to focus on one or the other. *The peoples of the new lands…*when had Europeans come to Nova Scotia? How had the Mi'kmaq fared then? She remembered studying their cultural artifacts, visiting a museum once when she was young. She and Mehron had brushed off the differences, for the most part, preferring to enjoy the modern sensibilities they had in common rather than those that set them apart. But now…

Her body felt tired. She pushed off the binder with the essay and fell back against her pillows. Her gaze landed on the wall above her desk, where her bodhràn still sat. She hadn't touched it for a week. She gazed, feeling sleepy, and closed her eyes. The shape of the drum stood out against the white wall, transferred to black on her eyelids. The after-image faded, but Dulci felt a wrinkle form between her brows as she concentrated on it. Her blood pulsed under her eyelids, sounding like a slow timbre of a drumbeat.

She opened her eyes again and crawled over to the foot of the bed. She stood up on the bed to reach the drum and took it down. Settling back again, she traced the outer rim with her finger, tapping lightly. She withdrew the tipper from the back. She held it above the edge, poised to strike, wondering what would happen.

It was the right thing to do. She would see something that would help Jesse. Taytere might tell her that he would protect Kukuwi and she wouldn't die this time… or no. How would that work? Could history be changed? Her hand drew back to hover over the history binder. *It felt like the right thing to do.*

She clacked the two ends of the tipper on the edge of

the drum, feeling with her other hand the back side of the skin, and the vibrations through it. She kept it light so that it wouldn't be heard downstairs, as she was certain her parents would forbid it. She ran the tipper over the entire round, stretching the time and slowing it down to a deeper pitch. She heard a fiddle in her mind, and was picking up her pace to match it, when the room disappeared.

She stopped drumming. She was sitting on snowy ground again, looking up at a hill, and it was nighttime. Snowflakes drifted down, with an occasional gust to make them swirl and scoot. She had on only her pajama pants and a sweatshirt, and none of her blankets had come with her, so she immediately felt the cold. But she didn't feel rooted to the ground as she had before. She would have to move and find somewhere that was shelter.

Before she could consider which direction to head, she heard a muffled shuffling in the snow. She looked up the rise and saw the glow of a light coming from behind it. Hope leapt up in her heart: *help*! Dulci thought. She scrambled up from her seat and trudged through the drifts to get to the top. It was less icy and more powdery snow than she remembered from the other visions. The night was still and the snow cloaked everything in a soft hush. Dulci felt the fear leave her as she reached the crest, and the ground under her feet leveled out. She stopped to wait for the owner of the light to reach her. All she could see was the oil lamp, swinging to and fro, in front of a leather-glove-clad arm. *Wait. No.*

The figure neared and Dulci could see the light glint ing off of reddish-blond hair, visible under the fur-lined hood of a long cloak. He got bigger and closer and Dulci knew who it must be. *Angus MacDonald.*

Would he see her?

Apparently he was aiming for the crest of the hill too, because he was making straight for her. His eyes followed his path strictly. He stopped about six feet away and patted the front of his coat. After this pause, he looked forward again. That's when he saw Dulci. He put up his lamp to get a better look, and she saw the blonde eyelashes covering his eyes, his reddened cheeks, the strong, broad brow. *Yep, definitely a relative of Finn's.*

"Hello," he said, unsure.

"Good evening," she replied, wanting to show him she was more civilized.

He looked taken aback at that, then smiled. "Evening," he said. "And what are you finding to do, past midnight on Indian Hill?" he asked conversationally.

"I—that is my business," Dulci replied formally.

"Without a light?" Angus asked, dubious. He saw her shiver. "And without warm clothing?"

"What are you doing out here then?" she asked to head off more questions about herself. Was Kukuwi nearby? Did Angus have the knife with him?

"Well, and that would be my business, would it not?" He smiled again, a little less openly.

Dulci huffed. What was she supposed to do here? He seemed like a different person, a cool-headed, if stubborn, one. Where was Taytere? That's who she needed to talk to, if she wanted to help Jesse.

"I am near Glace Cove, aren't I?" Dulci asked.

"Aye, 'tis just down the hill. They're all abed though now, 'tis all." His expression grew more wary. Her presence unexplained, her knowledge of her location questioned—he might well wonder if she was in her right mind.

"Well," Dulci decided to go for it. She had to find Kukuwi and Taytere and make sure they were all right, before she could figure out what to do while she was *here*. "Do you know where the Mi'kmaq village is?" She didn't want to draw him directly to the brother and sister though.

His eyes narrowed. "Why?"

"I have friends there I am seeking."

"Ah. Well." He hesitated. What was he thinking? For someone who hated that tribe, he didn't look at all perturbed. *Probably because he's a psychopath,* thought Dulci. *Stay alert.*

"I have friends there as well. I could take you there come the morning." *He has Mi'kmaq friends? What the heck? He's gotta be lying.* He cleared his throat. "Perhaps I should introduce myself. My name—"

"You're Angus MacDonald."

His eyes jumped. "Aye. And you are?"

"I am—I'm a traveller."

He waited. She decided to keep pressing.

"And I know you're going to do something very wrong. Or have done it already. I don't know which." At that strange statement, Angus looked at her hard. He held the lamp up closer to her face, and examined her. Hair, head, sweatshirt, thin cotton pajama pants, slippers. Ooh, she'd forgotten what she was wearing. A cold draft of air made her skin get goosebumps and she shivered again. He looked up. "Are ye a witch? Though we're no' but a wee slip of a girl, I'd list to a witch."

Dulci's brow puckered. What was he saying? *1777. He's from 1777.* This must be how they talked back then.

"It is 1777, right?"

"Aye." He lowered the lamp, giving both of them a queer, lit-from-below, ghost-story look.

"Did you do it yet?"

"I'm about to, this night. But I've thought it through; 'tis the only way to find a home for us both. It's not the intervale I'm seeking, only a bit of upland land to survive on. Have mercy!"

"Find a home? For who?"

"For Kukuwi and myself. There's no other land near the town not spoken for, and I'll not save enough for more land after I let my settlement acres go to waste—"

"Whoa—wait a minute. What are you going to do ton—I mean, this night?"

He stared steadily at her. "I mean to tear down the treaty sign for t'other side of Indian Hill. I know someone who will be happy to let it go to a white settler, so he'll change it in the city records. And then we'll have a wee spot of land to farm on, and grow on, and—"

"But that's wrong!"

"The Indians dinna use it. And I would make it productive, clear some of the forest, make a respectable steading, and all so that she will be safe!"

"Who?"

"Kukuwi."

What?

"You can't steal the land. It'll get all the Mi'kmaq kicked out!"

"Kicked out?"

"Her whole family will have to leave the Cove because of what you're doing." *And she's going to die, somehow*, she thought, but didn't say yet.

"They can go rot in bloody hell for all I care!" Angus was now huffing angrily. The next moment, he brushed past her and continued along the ridge, heading for a wooden post on the side of the hill. She hadn't noticed it before, but he must have been making right for it when she arrived.

"Angus, don't! Don't do it." She jumped through the powdery snow after him, following the shadow blocking the light.

He didn't speak to her, but kept walking. Twenty paces later, he stopped and drew a metal instrument from inside his cloak. A file or something. She saw the light glint on the metal as he set down the lamp. He took the file or crowbar or whatever it was in his hand, and angled it behind the sign. He set immediately to sawing at the nails holding the sign to its post, the nails squeaking through the wood audible to Dulci. It fell to the ground and he viciously scored the front of the sign with the sharp end of his tool, shredding whatever was attached.

Individual ribbons of vellum sprung up against the sign, which he tore off.

"Angus, stop! You don't know what's going to happen!"

"And ye do? We none of us do, Miss Traveler. I am protecting my new daughter." As he said this, his spine straightened and he seemed to grow even taller. Dulci cringed back at the fierce expression in his eyes, and a wind blew harder between them, making her eyes water.

"But it will kill her," she said softly. Angus affected not to hear, continuing his sawing, until she repeated it, running down through the snow drifts and grabbing the pieces of vellum that were left of the treaty proclamation. She grasped the wood in his hand and planted her feet as if to take it from him. "It will kill her!"

"No! They will kill her, if I can't protect her. They're angry she's left them. They threaten a riot on the toon— but we're doing all right. Kukuwi has been my salvation." He stopped and looked at her, his free hand closing over hers on the wood. His touch was not as threatening as she had expected, but gentle. "I thank'ee for coming. But I must do this for her, for us. Now ye must go, Traveler."

Her hand stayed on the wood as he let it go, and she stared at him. The lamp still lit up his features from below, and Dulci wondered which side she was supposed to be on now. "Angus, please. Don't."

"Ye mun go, and let me to my work this night." His voice grew in volume and ferocity. "Go!" He turned from her, pulling the wood away from her grasp, getting ready to nail his own version up in its stead. Dulci's fingers still clung to the pieces of scored, soaked vellum. She couldn't read what was on it, but knew it must be vitally important if she'd been thrown back here, exactly *now*. How could she stop him? He wouldn't listen to her, she couldn't stop him physically. The cold came back to her again, and in her hands she sensed the tipper coming back. *No*. She was going *back*. Or rather, *forward*.

"Angus, don't do it. Final warning!" she called, but she was already slipping away. He threw up an arm to ward away where she had been, and the next Dulci knew, she was lying on the floor next to her bed, one hand on the ground, one clutching a very moldy, cobwebby splinter of deadwood attached to several decaying scraps of vellum.

I failed. She rolled out the vellum, pressing it down gently to try and read it, but her tears blurred the vision. She pushed it to the side and curled up into a ball.

I failed.

Chapter 17

* * *

Waking up the next day was slow and achy. Neither of her parents had come up to check on her, so she'd been shivering. Her muscles ached from the shivering and her bones ached from the night on the hard floor. She blinked a few times, the sleep sticking in her eyes, before finding her clock. 4:31.

She uncurled and tentatively stretched her back. *Ow.* She moved to stand up and saw the scrap of wood and vellum near her hand again. She picked it up, then let the musty old corner of the sign drop back onto the floor. She wiped her hand on her leg, and climbed into her bed. She curled up under the blankets, then remembered her muscles. She stretched out and lay flat, willing her breath to fill the cramping places and calm them down. Her hand still felt dirty.

She woke again. Looked at the clock. 5:17. She turned over. Would this night never end? She didn't want to think about what would happen. What *had* happened. She practiced thinking about lapping water, the soothing waves. That made her have to pee. She got up and went to the toilet, came back, and lay flat again. Waves. Water. Out to sea.

* * *

When she woke again at 5:59, she resigned herself to the waking state. Her failure made tears prickle and her throat catch at odd moments while she got dressed and made her bed. It was still dark, but somewhere in town there were people rising, starting work, having breakfast. How could they bear it? Her stomach felt like it was lead-lined. She wanted to just stay in bed all day, but she couldn't hide forever. That's what she was doing, hiding from whatever power was sending her the visions. But as she remembered that she could just as easily have a vision in there, she felt the watery lump rise in her throat again, and choked out a sob.

Then a thought hit her like a lightning bolt. *If I failed, does that mean it's over? No more visions?*

She thought of Finn then, and what would happen to the two of them now if she was back to normal, but something had soured in that direction. He hadn't believed her. He'd told her she was weird. He'd let her down. Maybe he wasn't the ticket to happiness she'd thought. Where was her happiness, then?

She liked doing well at school, but that was suffering from her *weird*ness at the moment. She loved playing music, but she wasn't allowed, at least until the *weird*ness went away. She had a best friend, but couldn't go visit her house; more *weird*ness there.

No happiness, then. Well, that was fine. She didn't feel like being happy right now anyway.

She drew her knees up under the blankets and hugged them close. It was the position she'd seen Jesse in when she went into his room. Was that only two days ago?

She'd have to tell them. Jesse and Joan. And Mehron, if she would listen. The whole story. What would she use to convince Mehron? She knew she would just block it out. Her eyes fell to the crusty skirl of vellum and its attached splinter of wood. She'd bring it over to the house and tell them.

Today was what? Saturday? Yes. She'd go for a walk

and visit the Tebneks'.

* * *

She decided on a bowl of cereal: the light crispy one instead of oatmeal, since her stomach still felt full of chain mail. Her mother was scouring work papers over her coffee, readying for a full day of client counsel on the road. Her father was eating a bagel over his newspaper. When she entered, they both looked up, asked her how she'd slept, watched her get her cereal, waited for her to say something, then went back to their reading. *Well, that was easy*, Dulci thought, a little relieved but also disappointed. That's how much they cared?

She let them off the hook. *They just don't know. If you don't believe, you don't know.*

"I'm going for a walk," she said. Her ability to affect nonchalance seemed indirectly proportional to her need to appear nonchalant. Her mother looked up.

"Oh? Where to?"

"Down to the wharf, I think. I was dreaming of the waves." Hoped she wasn't laying it on too thick.

"That should be nice and peaceful. Gonna take some pictures?" her dad asked.

"Maybe."

"OK, well, bundle up well then, if you're going to be out a while. They say there's a front coming in later today."

"I will."

* * *

Joan wasn't surprised to see her at the door. She ushered her in without a word, stepping back and beckoning her forward. Dulci sat on a chair from the kitchen, facing Joan and Mehron on the sofa. Tuotu was out fishing on the water with some friends.

"Jesse had a bad turn last night. Did you have another vision then?" Joan asked. Dulci glanced at Mehron's face. It was fierce and stone-like. She sat up tall but wouldn't look at Dulci. Joan must have explained.

"Mehron, I'm sorry I didn't tell you. I couldn't—"
Mehron turned to her then.

"Couldn't what? Couldn't tell me what was going on, so instead you ran to my mom, since yours doesn't believe you either?"

"No, she doesn't. And I didn't think you would either." Dulci was resigned, sad, but not bitter. Not toward Mehron, and not toward her parents. How could she be? It *was* crazy.

Mehron was silent again. Perhaps she was compelled to sit here by her mom. Or maybe she wanted to know in case anything helped Jesse. A snigger of pain sliced through her chest. She looked at Joan.

"I did have one last night. It was—it was bad. It was different. I could move around, and talk to—the people then." She gulped. "I talked to Angus MacDonald." Joan's sharp intake of breath. She leaned forward to place a hand on Dulci's. She looked at her eyes, and felt the lump rise in her throat.

"I failed, Joan. I told him not to steal the land—he was ripping down some sort of ownership stake—I told him not to do it, because of all the stuff that would happen, but he wouldn't listen. He said he was doing it for her—for Kukuwi!" She rushed through the words, looking to see what Joan might make of it.

"For—but—" Joan had trouble finding words. Obviously it didn't make sense to her either. Mehron was still looking determinedly to her left. None of them saw Jesse on the other side of the sofa, emerging from his room in the hallway to stand watching them, until he spoke.

"You have to stay away from Finn. That's what Taytere says, Dulci."

His hair was still all tangled. He was bent over, a hand on the arm of the sofa for balance or strength, she didn't know which. He was wearing scruffy clothes, they might have been his pajamas, she couldn't tell. He smelled of unwashed, sweaty adolescent boy. But more than that, his sweat smelled like fear. Dulci could see it in his eyes too.

"Why doesn't he tell me then? Why only you?"

"Who is Taytere?" Mehron cut in.

"Kukuwi's older brother," Joan said.

"And what—"

"Hold on. Jesse, why stay away from Finn? Dulci's probably only involved because she's the link between you two. If she failed, it's over."

Dulci blinked. She was the link, the link to bring together the MacDonalds and the Tebneks. That's why Finn had felt drawn to her. Not attracted at all. Not interested in her as a person. She let out a whimper, then sniffled loudly to cover it. *Mustn't give in to it*, she thought. *Happiness will come back.*

She saw Finn's red-gold hair, a few strands floating over his eyes, his open blue eyes inviting her in. Happiness?

Mehron spoke again, this time in a low voice, firmly. "Jesse, go back to your room and leave us alone." Jesse turned to her, an incredulous look on his face. Joan was torn.

Finally she nodded and touched Jesse's hand. "Why don't you go back to rest, sweetheart. We need to discuss some things."

He calmed down from his bristling and looked at Dulci again. "Stay away from him, Dulci. I mean it."

She promised nothing, just watched him until he turned and shuffled down the hallway, hands following the wall for support. Pitiful.

"Dulci, you stay away from *him*," said Mehron, when he'd shut the door to his room. "I don't know what the *fuck* is going on, but he's gotten worse, and now you're getting it too. You stay away from him and things'll go back to normal. Right, Mom?"

"Mehron. I wish you were right. But I don't know. If that's the end, Jesse may just have to come to terms with his ancestor's presence somehow. If it's not..." Joan turned to Dulci again.

"If it's not, then maybe we'll get another chance. But for now," Dulci paused. She glanced toward the hallway, then back to Mehron, her voice lowering. "For now I agree, I don't think it's good for me to be around Jesse. We'll just have to see what happens."

She showed them the scrap of the post sign she had taken with her. Joan leaned forward to peer at it, trying to read the long-faded whorls of script, but did not touch it. Mehron looked at it with revulsion. *Something to fuel our delusions, she's no doubt thinking.*

"So what are you going to do about Finn?"

Dulci plumbed her depths. She was still feeling hurt from his treatment at the ceilidh the last time they'd talked, but she wanted to see if he could change his mind, maybe even like her for herself. That was it: she wanted to see if he was only drawn to her because of the curse.

"I'm going to ask him out on another date."

Mehron's expression was unreadable: somewhere between astonishment and confusion and pride.

Joan looked slightly worried, like she knew better why she needed to do this.

"Well, be careful," was all she said.

Dulci left the Tebneks' and paused outside to send Finn a text.

> **I've got a lot of catching up to do from being out sick. Midterms. Want to do a study date and then hot choc?**

The answer came a couple minutes later.

> **Sounds good. French midterm already on Mon. I hear u can help. ;) Pick u up tmw @noon?**

> **C u then**

Chapter 18

* * *

Study date. She accomplished nothing that morning. She thought about Jesse a few times, and his rebellious stance, those fierce eyes telling her to stay away from Finn. She felt sad about failing Jesse. But there was more to be known, which she could only discover by talking with Finn. If there wasn't, well, at least she was heading back toward normal. And she had to know whether it was the Fates messing with her or whether he really was interested in her, whether he'd really thought her pretty. *What a way to start high school*, Dulci thought.

The green pick-up roared up their driveway at 12:01. It was lashing rain after drizzling all morning. This was the front Olive had been talking about, a little late, but now determined to gloom up the last of their weekend. Olive answered the door, and Dulci came downstairs with all her materials in tow soon after. Finn was sitting on the sofa and her mom was perched on the edge of the rocking chair across from him. He had his book bag on the floor between his large feet. They both turned toward the stairs as Dulci paused on the last step.

"Finn was just telling me he made the hockey team, Dulci. Isn't that great news?" She turned back to him. "You know it's the hottest topic in this town, is hockey."

Finn made a noise that could have been agreement. He lifted his eyebrows in question to her. "So are we going to the same place? They were really nice, I wouldn't mind going back."

"Yeah, that's what I was thinking." She turned to her mom. "We'll be at APB in the Bell shops. I'm going to work on catching up on all my makeup assignments, and Finn's working on French." She gave him a brief smile. "So…bye, Mom."

"Bye, Mrs. Oyselle."

"Bye, guys. Work hard." She punctuated her last wry remark with a swing of her arm. Dulci rolled her eyes as they ran from the front door to the truck. They slammed their doors upon landing, already soaked and laughing at themselves. When Dulci turned to click in her seatbelt, Finn leaned over and kissed her temple. She lifted her head. He kissed her mouth, tugging on her lip a little. She'd closed her eyes, and waited till it was over to open them.

"Any better?" Finn asked, seeing her expression, and smiling a crooked smile.

She let out her breath in a rush. "Yes. But—" Dulci put her cold hands on his neck and pulled him back toward her. She canted her head like she'd seen people do in movies. She sucked on Finn's lower lip, lingered with a kiss at the side of his mouth, then pulled away slowly.

Finn's eyes were still closed. He collected himself, straightening his neck, licking his lips, and opening his eyes. *There was that genuine smile again*, thought Dulci. *Finally.*

"Ready?" she asked, feigning an innocent shrug.

"Ready," he replied with a grin, starting the motor and switching the wipers to their top speed.

* * *

Their table looking out onto the lake offered no distraction, since it was covered by fog and crisscrossed by storm clouds. The table itself was soon covered in books and papers, index cards, ruler, and calculator. An hour had passed, and Dulci had moved from science to literature, and was now on history. Finn rewarded each subject's conclusion with a kiss. He was still making his French flash cards.

Dulci's mind drifted back to the last time she'd been studying history and thinking of Finn... she'd outlined her answer to the question about which people of the New World had fared the best and the worst, and was now writing up the essay. She steadily pushed out of her mind any thoughts of Angus and his lies about stealing the Mi'kmaq land because he cared about Kukuwi. That made no sense, anyway. Did she dare ask Finn what he thought?

Her stomach dropped at the memory of what had happened last time. How thoroughly he'd rejected her. How small she'd felt when he'd dismissed her...affliction. *Maybe not.*

When she finished the essay a half-hour later, she put down her pen and waited for another minute before Finn realized she'd taken a break. He was concentrating fiercely on his textbook. Time for a test.

"Qu'est-ce que tu voudrais faire cet après-midi?"

His eyes, which had brightened upon seeing her take a break, anticipating another make-out session, dimmed. *"Qu'est-ce que* what?"

"What would you like to do this afternoon?"

"Oh. Are you done?"

"No. But I'm quizzing you." Dulci smirked. See how he liked being put under the gun.

"Uhhh...*Je voudrais*..." he searched for something he knew how to say. *"Je voudrais, te baiser!"* He looked triumphant.

Dulci exploded into laughter, having guessed the mistake that might pop up. "I think you meant *t'embrasser,"* she said, still giggling, and gave him the kiss.

"But *bisou,* and *baiser*..." She shook her head. "What's

baiser mean?"

"A lot more than *embrasser*, okay?"

His mouth formed an *O* and he looked down, his ears turning red. She caught a sideways glance and a small smile that let her know maybe he knew the joke. She scoffed. He smiled and cleared his throat. "So did you finish the history essay?"

Dulci sighed. This was definitely more comfortable, more normal. She nodded and he leaned across the table, placing his hands on a notebook. She heard the crinkling of a corner of a textbook page. By now he'd slipped his tongue into her mouth a few times, and while she didn't think it felt good, she at least didn't recoil. Suspended moments of that passed; she leaned back first. "How far are you then?" She wiped her mouth with the back of her hand. Wet kisses.

He sat back, imitating ecstasy for comic relief. "A third of the way through the chapters that are on the quiz. Hey," he changed his voice. "Talk more French to me. It sounds so sexy."

A thrill went through Dulci. Was this real? Was this really him saying she was sexy? Did it mean it was real, and not some magnetic force exerted by an ancestor's curse? She threw that last thought away and scrambled for something to say that would sound cool in French.

"*Je pourrais dire n'importe quoi, tu sais.*" She saw his blue eyes narrow at her inane comment; they focused on her mouth. "*Par exemple, le fait que tu es un beau gars, and que moi, je ne suis qu'une…*" She'd called him a cute boy, but groped for some word to describe herself. "*Une petite fille. Perdue dans le monde.*" She pictured herself, a little girl lost in the world, floating between the worlds she knew, that of school and Finn and her parents; and that of 1777, of Kukuwi and Angus and Jesse.

She closed her eyes, still feeling the floating sensation. It was dispelled when she felt Finn sit down next to her on the bench seat. He grabbed the back of her head and planted his mouth on hers, his other hand kneading her waist, creeping up…

"Hey!" She pushed his hand away and drew back her head. He opened his eyes. They were soft around the edges, so that he looked either sleepy or what she supposed was drunk. "Are you drunk?"

Finn blinked a couple times, drew back himself. "What?"

"You look so weird, like you're sleepy, or drunk. Like people on TV anyway."

Finn went from confusion back to happy contemplation. "No. Just turned on."

"Oh," said Dulci. *So* that's *what that looked like? Ugh. Weird.* "Well, I think it'd be better if you stayed on the other side of the booth."

"Okay. No problem." He snapped her a quick kiss on the cheek, making her jump a fraction, before reseating himself.

She was still a little shaken. *Just be in the moment? Or maybe we should work on French for a while. I can't concentrate anymore.*

"Maybe I can take a break from my makeup assignments for a while and quiz you on your flash cards?"

"Okay." He gathered them into a pile and handed them over. "Maybe we can order those hot chocolates now then, as a mini-reward?"

"YES," she said, agreeing readily, and grabbing at another normal ritual.

Ψ Ψ Ж

The whipped cream was long gone, and the hot chocolate was reduced to cold pools in the bottoms of their mugs when at last Dulci tackled math. Finn had all his vocabulary written out and could start quizzing himself with it.

It was 3:49 and the rain had turned to sleet, the sky steel-grey with it. No more thunder and lightning though, just the rhythmic waves of pounding slush on the roads and sidewalks. Dulci stared at the thirty problems she had to draw. Groaned. Finn glanced at the graph paper she was working on and passed her the protractor. "You're already in Geometry?"

"Yeah, we had an early-track math group at the grade school." Dulci yawned. Right angles. She could do that.

"That's pretty cool."

She heard the grudging respect in his tone. "What math are you in?"

"Advanced Algebra. It sucks."

Dulci smiled to herself. *Boys are such weenies,* she thought.

Finn looked at his watch. "Almost four. Wanna do another half an hour then head back? I don't wanna drive with too much crap on the roads."

"Sure," she said, glancing out the window to the lake again. *Steel. Jagged heartbeat waves all across the water. No nice sine or cosine waves.* She smiled again to herself. *Math joke!*

Working steadily through her graphs, she eyed Finn from time to time. He was scrunching up his forehead, closing his eyes, biting his lip. Apparently French vocabulary *was* really hard for him.

When they got back in the truck, soaked instantly again, she gave him one kiss, then grabbed his book bag and pulled out his flashcards. She quizzed him on their slow, careful drive back to her place. When he stopped at the bottom of her driveway, she set her hand on the door handle and looked back at him.

"Sorry, I don't want it to slip on that steep angle," he said. "Could take out your fence!" He was teasing her.

"It's okay. I wasn't drenched enough anyway," and she stuck her tongue out at him. She jumped out, running for the house. Only when she got to the safety of the door did she turn around and watch as he negotiated a three-point turn and headed out. She was grinning as she stepped inside to stamp her feet in the mudroom before taking off her shoes.

Her dad poked his head in from the living room. "You've got a visitor," he said. He sounded uptight, Dulci noticed. He couldn't have seen her locking lips with Finn in the truck though, not at the bottom of the driveway. *Ah, so that's why he did that*, Dulci realized belatedly. *Duh.*

She shook off the water from her coat, hung it on a peg, and entered the living room.

Mehron was there. She sat on the sofa, spine straight but seeming to quiver. She didn't look up as Dulci came in and sat on the rocking chair, and Dulci saw she was troubled by something. Scared, even.

"Hey," Dulci said softly. "How'd you get here in this weather?"

"Dad drove me over."

"What's up?"

"Did you just get back from—Finn?"

"Yeah," she said, feeling a little guilt creep back in from enjoying herself when she should have been trying to save Mehron's brother. "Why? I was going to tell you about it at school tomorrow, you know. I'm all caught up to go back to school, it was a study—"

"Did you talk about…all the vision stuff? Did he say anything about Jesse or a curse or anything?" Her face was strained, anxious.

"Not really. It didn't go over too well last time I tried that. Why? Has something happened?"

"Sort of. Not really. Jesse's just—he's crying, and screaming, there's lots of your name in there now too." She met Dulci's gaze, her dark eyes large and scared. "I was just hoping you'd know something more. I hate it— I hate our house like this."

Dulci wanted to reach out to give her a hug, but she was so wound up she thought she might explode. "Wanna go upstairs?"

Mehron nodded and headed up the stairs to Dulci's room. Dulci followed, after grabbing a box of Oreo cookies from the top of the fridge.

Mehron was sitting on the edge of her bed when she got there, and accepted an Oreo with a small smile. "Your mom hates these," she said.

"I know, but Dad lets me have 'em every once in a while," Dulci said. She sat against her pillows, facing her friend, wondering how she could make her feel better. "What does your dad think about all this stuff?" she asked.

Mehron pushed her eyebrows up and blew out a small breath. "He's just pretending it doesn't happen and going away when it gets really bad. Working. My mom is the one who's taking care of Jesse, mostly. And by that I mean giving him food and water when he doesn't remember to eat. Sometimes I think when he zones out, we're just *gone*, to him… we could walk back into his room and find a skeleton."

Dulci tried to hide the shiver that her words produced. "That's rough. It's kind of what my parents are doing. They're just denying it happened. Telling me I must be dreaming. My mom even asked me if I was on *drugs*."

"Pah!" That got a surprised pop of laughter from Mehron. She shook her head, agreeing how absurd that was.

"They also told me I couldn't do any extracurriculars because I must be so *stressed out*. So, no music."

"Oh, no, seriously? How… how can they think that has anything to do with it?"

"Cuz I told them I was drumming the first time it happened." Dulci lowered her voice. "And then it happened again. I tried drumming to make it happen, right here, and it did!" Mehron edged away from the bodhràn sitting on the shelf.

"I still don't want to believe it's happening. Especially since you didn't tell me…"

"I know. I'm sorry. I just didn't want to worry you, with Jesse getting worse, and it being related to that…

we'll figure it out, and then everything will go back to normal. I want to promise it, but I can't." Dulci's eyes were filling again. "I can only try. And if I fail, try again." Should she tell Mehron about her failure? She hadn't had time to tell Joan the details when she'd last visited. Would that help? Or just make it worse for Mehron?

She was just about to start the story, when Mehron slipped off the bed to look at something on her desk. "What's th—" She picked up the chunk of rotted wood with a stiff scrap of something attached. *The property sign.* Before Dulci could explain, Mehron's hands grasped it as if electrified. Her arms shot out, like she was trying to hold it away from herself. She turned her head, as if it was sending out a heat that she couldn't take.

"Mehron? Mehron? What are you—"

It was only a few seconds. Before Dulci could finish her thought, it was over, and Mehron collapsed, like all her bones had turned to water. She crumpled to the ground, knocking her head on the edge of the desk as she fell.

"Hey!" The shout did nothing to revive her, but it did bring Dulci's dad up from where he'd been talking with Tuotu.

"Dulci, what's the matter?" He watched her go to Mehron's side on the floor. "Is she sick? Here, let me see." Dulci scooted aside from her friend, her doubting, normal friend, who was now probably trapped in some plane of time, no idea what was going on. It was *not* a faint. *She'd been taken.* But she couldn't tell Dad that. As he checked Mehron's vital signs, she edged toward the desk and grabbed the wood, keeping it behind her back. She edged over to her closet, then thrust it into an empty shoe box. Don was listening to her breath, and finally looked back at Dulci. "Call an ambulance! She's unconscious and not responding."

Dulci ran into her parents' bedroom and nearly knocked the phone over when she grabbed for the receiver. She checked the cord was still in the socket before calling 9-1-1. *Ohmygod, ohmygod, ohmygod. What do I do now?* Dulci talked to the dispatcher while her mind was skipping down another track. After confirming her address with them, she hung up, then immediately dialed the Tebneks' number. Joan answered. Dulci mumbled, "It's Dulci."

"What's happened? Jesse just went stock-still, and I can't get a word out of him. He looks scared to death. Mehron's with you, right?"

Tears clogged Dulci's throat and made her speech garbled. "She's here, but she's not all right. We called an ambulance—"

"What happened? Oh dear God. Not both of them. Christ Almighty…"

Dulci couldn't speak. *Sorry*, she thought at the phone, but couldn't blink the tears out of her eyes. "We'll take her to St. Ann's. Meet you there?"

"Yes, I'll—we'll—I don't know what to do. With Jesse. Oh God, Tuotu. Where is he? Is he still with you?"

"Yeah, he's downstairs, I think."

"Okay. I'll—figure something out. Meet you at St. Ann's." A micro-pause. "It's not your fault, Dulci." Then the click, and the line was dead.

Dulci stood in her parents' bedroom, the phone hanging from her hand, until her dad shouted for her help. She put the phone back in its cradle, and wiped her face with the backs of her hands. Her dad was calling for some cotton from the bathroom, so she went and got that, all the while feeling in a daze and numb to other sounds. She came back into her own room with the cotton and the alcohol disinfectant, and watched as her dad turned Mehron's body on its side and dabbed at a place above her temple with it. Blood. Not much. But blood.

Dulci felt the sensations of the past come back to press against her—the fog, the howling, chill wind—but clung tightly to her cloud of numbness. She knew what the failure to change Angus' mind had felt like. She didn't want to feel the pain of this.

Chapter 19

* * *

Tuotu took the news more calmly than Joan had. Dulci and Don rode in the ambulance with him. The emergency responders worked away at helping Mehron breathe, beating her heart for her, and listening, all the trip to the big hospital, which lasted twenty interminable minutes. Don sat to one side, furiously texting on his phone, probably to her mom, and Dulci sat next to him, her hands balled together in a fist in front of her mouth and biting nervously on her thumbnail. She never did that. Good thing her mom wasn't here.

The numbness was still there. She had several images vying for attention in her cloud though: that shoe box with the wooden fragment of the sign, Joan's voice on the phone when she'd said 'It's not your fault, Dulci,' and Angus' angry face as she'd tried to stop him. Fail, fail, fail.

They got to the hospital and were separated, Don and Dulci watching as Mehron's stretcher was attached to a gurney and wheeled off down the hallway, with Tuotu walking alongside. They disappeared behind double doors and harsh lights that blinded.

Joan found them in the hospital's small waiting room for emergency some minutes later. Joan's hair was flying every which way, and her bright quilted clothing, which usually made Dulci feel cozy and at home, was askew and covered with a big navy blue windbreaker. The edges of her apron peeked out below its hem.

In answer to her unasked question, Don spoke. "She's in emergency, and they just told us to wait. She had a small knock on the head, but nothing else they could find wrong. She just stopped breathing. I couldn't get her to start—I'm sorry, Joan—"

Joan came to sit beside Dulci, and wrapped both arms around her, pressing her head to Dulci's ear uncomfortably. After a few moments like this, Tuotu emerged. "What'd you do with Jesse?" Dulci whispered to Joan.

"He's at home, and will stay until we get back."

Dulci remembered Mehron's words about Tuotu's denying what was happening. Well, he'd have to take notice of this. But since it wasn't her family, she let it go. An awkward silence descended on the group. Don, who felt embarrassed by his suspicion of Jesse and guilty because Mehron had had her accident in his home. Tuotu, who felt unable to talk to his good friend about a family problem that had been going on for years. Joan, who felt constrained talking about the visions in front of non-believers, or so Dulci imagined.

And Dulci? How did she feel? Hungry. And cold.

* * *

She huddled in the waiting room for a long time, deeply aware of the humming sound all the electronics made. The soda machine, the silent TV, the water cooler. The harsh light that blinded her every time she opened her eyes. The goings-on of other occupants: Tuotu and Joan had gone back in together as soon as the doctor came out to say that they'd done all the preliminary tests on Mehron and were awaiting the results of a few of them, while she was on a life support machine. Her dad had left to fetch food for the Tebneks, since it was apparent Joan had been cooking dinner when she'd gotten the call.

The only other occupant of the waiting room at present was a girl named Maeve. She was a sophomore at Glace Cove High, as far as Dulci knew, and hadn't volunteered information on why she was there or even greeted Dulci when she came in. She didn't care. She wanted to leave. Find a down comforter and wrap herself up in it. Devour a whole pizza. Fit her hands around a mug of hot chocolate. Share a hot chocolate with Mehron again. God, how had they taken her? Why was Angus reaching through time to get at another victim? He had seemed so gentle when they'd talked, but then frightfully fierce. Which type of person was he? How could she know for sure? She felt furious enough about Mehron to go back with the piece of the treaty sign at home and run to the city fathers and expose him. Only who would believe her then? About as many people as believed her now, she imagined.

If it helped to be mad at Finn, she would do that, but he seemed so thoroughly out of it, out of the loop of everything, that she doubted it would. But so had Mehron, so why was she now stolen away from under Dulci's nose? The electronic noise faded away as Dulci worked through the logic of it. If Angus killed Kukuwi and Taytere cursed him, why isn't Finn the one in trouble? *Why does he seem so innocent?* A blockhead maybe, when it came to dates and understanding girls, but innocent in terms of this family history of revenge.

And Kukuwi had come to her for help, before she was killed, but not about Angus. She'd said it was about the land and her family. Could she have been that far off-track? Somehow, Dulci felt like the young girl wouldn't have been able to talk to her across time if she'd been so wrong about her own situation. Weren't ghosts supposed to be all-knowing?

She'd felt so awful when she'd failed to stop Angus stealing the Mi'kmaq land. She'd failed to protect Kukuwi, a sweet young girl who'd probably never hurt a fly. And she'd failed Jesse, her best friend's brother, by not removing the curse. From where she sat now, her failure seemed even worse: Mehron was now being held captive by the forces she was battling against, blind and ill-equipped.

When the doctors next came out, the male doctor looked around for Don, but seeing he was gone, he conferred with the female doctor and she left. He sat down next to Dulci. "Is your dad due back soon?"

"Yeah. He went out to get some food for Joan and Tuotu."

"Well, that was very nice. You know, they're kind of rattled right now. While we're waiting for the test results, we have no idea what's wrong with Mehron. I was hoping you could fill us in on some of the details that might help. Such as, what were you guys doing when she fell?"

"We—she—we were in my room talking. I was on my bed, and Mehron got up to look at something on my desk. She started to say something, then just collapsed. She hit her head on the edge of my desk, but it didn't look like it was really hard. My dad came in right away, so she wasn't out for long before he started with the CPR. Can you tell if she has brain damage or anything?" *God, please no. Please let it be just temporary.*

"Well, we did get a scan of the brain because we were concerned with the reaction based on such a small bump, but it came up pretty normal. We can't agree on what might be happening right now."

"Oh." *Well then, you're not helping much, are you?* Trouble was, she couldn't help much from here either.

"Thing is, Dulci, Mr. And Mrs. Tebnek are pretty scared. They're not able to see anyone right now, while they're dealing with the shock. Do you know what I'm saying?"

"They don't want to see me."

"I'm afraid not. I'm sure it'll pass in a few hours, or maybe overnight." At this point, Dulci caught sight of her dad, coming through the hallway with two large white paper bags. Olive followed behind, with a tray of drinks. "Don! Olive," he said as her parents came over. They listened to the same few lines from the doctor, and handed over the food, to be given to the Tebneks in the private room where they were waiting with Mehron. They thanked the doctor and bundled Dulci into the car. Olive had come back from her daily appointments in time to get Don's texts and pick him up so they could swing by the Pasta Pita. They now headed right back out, Don looking glad to be spared the meeting with his friend for the moment.

Back home, Dulci felt the cloud of numbness melting. She was back on familiar territory, and every familiar thing sung out its recrimination. Her backpack on its peg: no more school with Mehron. The living room sofa: where she'd seen Finn on their first date, sitting with her mother. The edge of her desk: the last time she'd heard Mehron speak. Her bodhràn on its shelf: the menace of the past reaching out to grab the people she loved.

A wave of hatred for what was happening to her, resistance to this destiny, rose from her stomach to her chest and threatened to escape out her throat, so she threw herself onto the bed and screamed into her pile of pillows. After only a few breaths, the screams turned into sobs. She felt her face getting hot from the lack of air but continued crying, the hatred and frustration coming out like tearing seams until she finally floated away into the oblivion of exhaustion.

* * *

She woke while it was still dark. A glance at her phone showed her the glowing digits 3, 5, and 2. The grey storminess of yesterday's study session had yielded to a quiet dark. Monday. It was Monday. School. Would she go to school? Did it matter?

What was her purpose now? Did she still have a chance to change the past? Maybe she had simply gone to the wrong moment, and she needed to go further back?

Make sure that Kukuwi and Angus never met? Yes! Why hadn't she thought of it before? A brief flash of Kukuwi returning to the hill house crossed her mind, but she put it aside, along with the effects of the curse, under Things That Don't Make Sense About The Past. It might get to be a long list. But at least she had an idea of how to help Mehron, and Jesse, and Kukuwi. *Normal* with Finn would have to wait, if it ever had a chance.

Dulci got on the bus with the other students, paying no attention as one or two of them looked and muttered to one another. She supposed they'd already heard something of the news from that sophomore, Maeve, but it set the tone for her day: ignore, ignore, ignore. Maybe she could even ignore the teachers. For her plan, she only needed to be allowed to drum herself into the past. She'd woken to find her bodhràn gone from its shelf. Not unexpected. If they couldn't believe her, they certainly couldn't trust her to follow their rules anymore. Still, it hurt, this shattering of the shell she had made for herself over many years. Untrustworthy. She felt like…less.

The first few classes, then break. The teachers had been surprised to see her, as they all knew by now of Mehron's illness, and that they were close friends. For break, she holed up in the girls' toilet, overhearing gossip just as Mehron had on that first day of school.

"They said she hit her head on some furniture, but what if Dulci pushed her?"

"But they're best friends! They'd have to be fighting over something big, like a guy…"

"Exactly. Finn MacDonald is the new guy, turns up looking for Dulci Nobody Freshman… what's that about?"

"I know. I thought he was really cute. Why would he have to go looking for Fresh Meat?"

Running water drowned out the rest of the conversation, which was a relief. She got out in time to change the books in her locker and walk to her next class, the words of the girls—obviously upperclassmen—ringing in her ears. She got to the corner nearest the door and almost bumped into someone coming around the other way. She mumbled an apology and snuck into science to get a seat at the back. The teacher didn't comment on the change from her usual place at the front, merely offered a pitying smile. She continued to ignore teachers, realizing they'd all conferred over break and decided to leave her alone. She wondered if Mr. McKenna was among that number.

Two periods later, it was time for lunch and she needed a better hiding place. She was thinking of the parking lot, even though it was pretty cold, when a warm presence at her right elbow made her turn and step back a bit. "Finn." Her voice was low, dead.

"Hey there. You look like death warmed over. What's wrong?"

Apparently he hadn't gotten the newscast. "What's wrong? You mean you haven't heard?"

He shook his head, leaning back visibly from her vehemence.

"Everything! Every fucking thing is wrong. Not just *weird*, Finn. Wrong. Mehron is in the hospital, my parents took away my bodhràn, Jesse's gone silent, and Kukuwi's still going to die! Unless I do something about it."

"Why is Mehron in the hospital?"

"Because she touched the guilt of the past!" When it came from Dulci's mouth, she gasped. "The curse! Do you believe the curse now, you freaking MacDonald? She's in a coma or something because of your ancestor—the least you could do is look guilty."

Finn didn't look guilty. He looked confused and scared and like he was going to run away. He tentatively put a hand out to her arm.

"Look, Dulci, I didn't mean—"

"I don't care! You haven't helped anything, so I'm going to just stay away from you. And you," she said, punctuating the word with her finger in his chest, "can stay away from me.

She turned and hurried through the hallway, finding her way to the stairwell and racing up it. Maybe she would just talk to Mr. McKenna now.

* * *

She got to Room 212 and knocked. "Come in," called a voice. It was he, looking a little less formal, but still wearing grey: a sweater today.

"Ah, Miss Oyselle. We missed you at our last meeting, but I'm sure we'd still love to have you in the group to help things along. We're proposing a short concert for the Thanksgiving assembly; what do you think?"

"I'd love to, Mr. McKenna." She almost felt like calling him Sir because of his stodgy dress and wisp of an accent. "But my parents don't think it quite the thing right now. My friend Mehron had an accident yesterday, you see, and I've been seeing things—"

"Oh, my dear, do sit down. I can see there's been something upsetting, to be sure, but music should help with that, not aggravate it."

"I know—I mean, I thought so too, but they don't agree—my parents." She ended with a sidelong glance at the box next to his desk, wondering if it contained the bodhràn she'd played here before. He read her glance and her defeated air with practiced teacherly intuition and walked over to the corner, waving her to sit alongside the desk, in one of the concert seats. He opened the box and handed her the bodhràn, then crossed the long room again to close the door.

"We've got plenty of time for lunch, Miss Oyselle. Let's see what we can do together." He went to the wall of windows and picked up a violin case, drawing out the same fiddle from before. *What, three weeks ago? Is it still September? No, the month had just turned: October.* Close to Thanksgiving and Halloween and Samhain. Dulci picked up the drum and tapped with her fingers on its rim. A sizzle went up her arm. Now was the time for her plan.

Think: before Angus and Kukuwi meet, before they meet!

She started drumming and repeated the phrase in her cadence: *before they meet, before they meet.* She heard Mr. McKenna's fiddle start a lilting tune, slow and light. It picked up and slid down to some lower notes. *Before they meet, before they meet.* Dulci closed her eyes and clenched the tipper harder before the wind rose up to overwhelm the violin. She opened her eyes and threw down the drum, stumbled to the wall of windows. Only it was now a tiny window looking onto the main road of a town. *Glace Cove? In 1777? How much earlier am I?*

Dulci peered around and saw the road littered with leaves, gold and red and brown. A stiff wind was swirling them about. There were several structures across from her, but whether houses or shops, she couldn't tell. Her own tiny window held a sign on which "OPEN," was carefully lettered, which meant it must read "CLOSED" to the passersby. Should she stay there, out of the wind? Or venture out onto the golden road?

Chapter 20

* * *

If it had worked, and she was back before 1777, she needed to find Kukuwi, and stick with her until she was out of danger. If not… well, how would she know? It looked like late afternoon by the light. Could she knock on one of the doors of the houses? Could she make her way to the south of town and still find a Mi'kmaq village there? Was there anyone here, at all?

The air was gentle for a moment, but then the autumn wind returned. It lashed the yellow birch branches to and fro. Dulci glanced the other way up the lane, still seeing no one. It was like the lane was beckoning her out of the small space, into the open. *In for a penny*, she thought.

She crept away from the wall, locating the door by the cracks of natural light coming through it. It squealed open under her hand, and she peeked out. Still no one. She turned to find the waterline at the bottom of the slight rise. She turned right, heading south.

Minutes passed as she walked. The air seemed to have been sucked out of the place. It was warm enough so that she didn't feel chilled in her t-shirt and fleece. After emerging from the the little row of houses, there was nothing for some way, just the lane. It had green grass growing in the middle of two cart tracks. She followed them for over a mile without seeing a soul. Trees bordered the hillside, many turning brilliant colors. She looked left toward the water and saw the same view she had from her window at home: the little peninsula into the bay, with a sloping depression just as it reached the mainland, like it was almost going to separate but had decided not to. She looked back to the hill. No house, just trees. One particular maple near the road, which rose about four feet.

Dulci caught her breath. *This is our tree, by the streetlamp. It is over two hundred years old.*

She felt the whirl of time changing, but shook her head, hurrying along down the road. That was not what she had come to see. *Keep going. Find Kukuwi.*

Around the bend of the hill, she saw on the flat part of the land a structure, a church. Ah! And there were all the people!

Dulci stepped behind a tree where she could observe the group of parishioners. There were about fifteen of them, and they were all standing in the meadow next to the church. There was a priest and another man standing alone, apart from the others. The priest wore a black suit: breeches, waistcoat, and a long-tailed coat. The other man wore rougher clothes: shabby chestnut-brown breeches and a shirt and coat of dark grey wool. He wore no wig like the others, but had his red-gold hair tied back in a queue. *Angus!*

Why was she here? Was she supposed to talk to him again? His face was pale and ravaged, lines carved into the cheeks from fierce grimaces of pain and terror. She'd already tried to talk to him, and he hadn't listened. But if it was before… should she tell him not to befriend any Mi'kmaq children? No—not only would she look crazy in her modern clothes, she would sound crazy. But who was he burying? What had Joan said about the Scots settler…

She hopped to another tree, trying to get closer but

remain unnoticed. One more, a large oak, and she could just barely hear some of the words being said.

"Though her time was short, the Lord lays claim to those he loves, and we must let them go. The blessed of this world…"

They were burying a woman. Now Dulci remembered: his wife had died.

"And we must not question the ways of the Lord, nay, but bide in His light and glory…Those she leaves behind must take comfort in His ways…"

Come on, keep going, she thought at the minister.

"And those who leave the bosom of the Lord for only a short time, may be assured mercy when they be but snatched back…"

Short time… the baby? *A wife and baby… she must have died in childbirth.*

Dulci's heart twisted for him, even though she knew what he would come to do, what he *had* done. Was his lashing out at Taytere rooted in his anger and grief over his wife and child? *Enough, get going.*

Dulci crept backward again, pressing her sneakered feet into the ground slowly to avoid calling attention to herself. When no one moved, she turned and continued along the path. Something brushed at the edges of her mind. She thought about the funeral she'd just witnessed, wondering when it might have taken place. *I must be here before the murder, but what am I witnessing? I can still find Kukuwi and make sure they haven't met yet. Then tell her to stay away from him.*

Jesse's voice rang out in her memory: *Stay away from the MacDonald boy.* Her heart skipped a beat. Was history repeating itself in her own time? It was so frustrating.

After the church there were no more structures for another quarter-mile, then she saw small wisps of smoke. They rose up through the pinkening sky, and she hoped it was the Indian settlement. She quickened her step and rounded the bend, turning down toward the water's edge. There they were: ceremonial wigwams the nearest structures, with longhouses and fire grounds between them. A few people were visible, wearing the leather clothes with simple embroidery and bead jewelry that she recognized. Where would she find Kukuwi? How old was she in this time?

She watched the action for a few minutes. A small knot of people was working, salting fish. Another knot was tending a large fire. A lone tall boy was walking from tent to tent, calling something to those inside. It was a hive of activity, compared to the still street of shops that she'd passed.

Dulci noticed a small figure coming toward her. The small child hid its face behind long straight black hair, baring only one eye to peruse Dulci and her strange clothing. Dulci stood without moving, bearing the the scrutiny patiently. She needed someone here who would talk to her about the village. Also, someone who spoke English. Or French. Dulci's breath caught. Were there still Acadians here?

"Y'a des Acadiens?" she asked in her best country French accent.

The child just stared back, but someone else's head perked up at her speech. It was an adolescent boy. He wore no shirt, just bead-decorated breeches and a sort of fur belt around his middle. He looked at them briefly then walked nimbly over from the tent where he'd been.

"Qu'est-ce qui'ya?" he asked for them both. *What's the matter.*

"Je cherche une fille. Elle s'appelle Kukuwi." The little girl looked up, curiosity intense in her liquid black eyes at hearing her name. The boy stood a little taller, stepping slightly in front of her.

"Et qu'est-ce que vous voulez?" *And what do you want. What, indeed?* thought Dulci.

"C'est elle?" She pointed to the girl behind him. It was her, of course, but she had no English and would not understand any warnings about a certain Angus MacDonald. Could she tell this older brother or cousin-type? He crossed his arms but nodded. "Et vous êtes Taytere, alors?"

His brows lowered, distrustful. "Comment vous savez ça? Oui, je m'appelle Taytere, et elle est ma soeur, Kukuwi." *How did she know it.*

Dulci didn't answer the question immediately, but looked at Taytere's eyes. Eventually the brows relaxed, and he looked calm again. How to get her meaning across? "Il faut la protéger," she said, pointing to Kukuwi again. *You must protect her.*

His forehead lowered again, in scorn. "C'est pas votre affaire." *It's none of your business.* Well, it would be. She decided to tell the truth and hope this boy was responsible for some of Joan's intuition and understanding.

"Je viens du futur." *I come from the future.*

He looked blank for a minute, then glanced at her clothes and around her at the empty lane. "Ça ne me regarde pas. Et nous, nous ne sommes pas votre affaire." *That doesn't concern me, and we're none of your business.*

He stepped closer to her then, after reaching behind him to push Kukuwi back. She wasn't expecting it, and fell on her bum. She parted the hair to look at Dulci again before getting up and dusting herself off. She walked away. Meanwhile, Taytere gave Dulci a hard look that clearly meant *Stay Away.* Her counsel to protect his sister hadn't exactly helped, had it? He'd just pushed her onto the ground. An accident, obviously, but not a good indicator of familial affection. What else could she say, if he didn't care that she'd come from the freaking future?

"Ne fais pas—" but before she could tell him what not to do, she felt a tugging sensation at her shoulder blades, and was being sucked backwards. No, she couldn't go back yet!

But it was done. She stood in the classroom again, holding the drum and tipper in her hands. Like before, Mr. McKenna was just turning his head. This time though, he squinted his eyes at Dulci. He put down his violin. "Has it happened again then?"

"What—yes." Dulci was trying to catch her breath, as it felt like she'd run all the way back from the Mi'kmaq settlement to the school. She sat, feeling her ears warm to the level of the heating inside, and hearing the echo of her words: ne fais pas… *Don't.*

"Would you like some water? The time travelers I've known usually got quite a headache when they returned…"

"The—what did you just say?"

"It happens to more people than just you, Miss Oyselle. The Fates manipulate and deceive any number of people, I'm told." After that extraordinary sentence, Dulci expected more. Could he tell her then, how to bring Mehron back? But he only stepped over to the podium to grasp his thermos and pour some water into the cup that perched on top. He offered it to her. Dulci glared at him, ignoring the cup.

"This is just too freaking weird. I can't even think straight. I just went "back," but accomplished nothing, as far as I can tell. Then I come back to someone who knows the whole story, and didn't help? Why didn't you tell me anything before?"

"The whole story? Dulci, I am merely a believer, not an all-knowing sage. You have to do what you have to do. It is for you to figure out." He paused delicately. *Such a delicate man*, Dulci thought spitefully. "Your friend Mehron is in hospital, yes? And she didn't believe?" Dulci nodded reluctantly. "Hmm. Are you the link then?" he inquired.

"Someone told me I was." *Jesse.*

"And he or she didn't elaborate?"

"He told me to stay away from Finn. But if I do, then I'm no longer the link, and he goes on suffering from migraines and visions forever! I can't do that."

"Hmm," he mused again. "Well, what does a link do, Miss Oyselle?"

"Connects two things together."

"It holds two things together, yes. Maybe your friend couldn't tell you what to do because he is being blinded by his own visions. Everyone only gets a piece of the picture, you know. It's why we have to work together."

Dulci shot him a glare. The 'we' rang false, as she'd only seen this teacher looking quite at ease, perfectly comfortable, in this very classroom. But Jesse, blinded by his visions? What did he mean? She'd talked to Taytere now too, and that's who Jesse saw. Should she go to the hospital, check to see if Mehron was—?

Her thoughts were interrupted by the bell ringing the end of lunch period.

"Ughh." The groan was triggered almost before she realized she was making a sound. Mr. McKenna had put the cup down on her desk.

"You might want to drink some water before you go to your next class. Just as a health precaution." He turned his back on her then and set to carefully putting away the violin.

Dulci would have sent knives from her eyes into his back if she'd been able, but she quickly turned away and slammed the drum onto the next desk. She grabbed her bag from the floor and ran to Geometry.

Chapter 21

*   *   *

The class passed in a blur and she was excused from suiting up for P.E. She sat on the bench, as she had often done these past few weeks. She watched the students in their uniforms run through warm-ups, then set up the orange cones for soccer drills. Her mind drifted. What could she make of that last vision? She was sure she'd gone before 1777, because Kukuwi had been there, maybe five years younger, and hadn't known any English yet. What had changed?

The funeral in the church cemetery. That had been Angus. She knew he was burying his wife and child, which was pretty awful. Not something he was likely to turn from and want to talk to some stranger about. How did he develop such a strong feeling about Kukuwi then? *What else was different?*

Was there something special about Mr. McKenna's classroom? She hadn't been there for anything but the music group lessons, so she didn't know what else happened in there. Toxic fumes. Formaldehyde from dead things in jars. Any number of things could have made him go crazy. But at least she hadn't, not yet. So was he part of all this too? Or just, as he'd said, a believer, like Joan?

Dulci chewed her lip. No, he wasn't like Joan. He knew more, for some reason. He'd talked with other time travelers, as he called them. But he didn't seem to want to help her. "Everyone only gets a piece of the picture," he'd said. Or puzzle. Something like that. Did Mr. McKenna have a piece? Did Finn?

She didn't want to go back up there. She needed a break, more information, before she attempted to go back again. She wanted to see Mehron again.

A soccer ball rolled over and stopped by her foot. She glanced up and noticed that the students had all gathered around the coach to turn in the balls and get high-fives. That meant school was almost over. She stood up, and felt the world go sideways. She put out a hand and landed awkwardly on her side on the bench. "Oof," she huffed as she tried to right herself without anyone seeing. She was dizzy just standing. She called out to Coach Johnson. He came jogging over and she had to ask for help getting back up the small hill to the school building. He volunteered to walk her back, and dismissed all the kids, who were looking around with curious stares.

Halfway up the hill the bell rang. About ten slow steps later, a lanky figure with red-gold hair was loping down the hill.

"Hi, Coach Johnson, I can help her the rest of the way."

"Well, sure," he said, glancing at Dulci for confirmation. No doubt he'd heard the new hockey recruit was going out with the weirdo freshman. Who *wasn't* talking about it? She nodded. "Thanks, Finn. Hope you feel better real soon, Dulci. Bye," he said, and strode off for his office. Finn put one hand on her back, and offered his other arm for her to grab hold of.

"I'm fine. I'm just thirsty. I think I'm dehydrated."

"No wonder. If I was blowing as much steam as you did back there, I'd be messed up too."

"Sorry I snapped at you," she not-so-graciously returned. "Clearly I *am* going nuts."

"Dulci, I'm sorry. I didn't know what happened with Mehron. Can you tell me about it? Did you think there was something I could do to help?" She looked up at him, shading her eyes from the sun that was backlighting him. His eyes were clear, his features taut with concern. For her? Or for himself? She would have to trust him.

"I need some water first."

He led her to the water fountains by the back entrance, and she took several long draughts before pausing to sit on a picnic bench and take a deep breath. She felt eyes on her, and turned to look up at the second floor of the school. In one window stood a figure with white curling hair and ruddy skin, looking their way. Dulci turned back and took another deep breath.

"I didn't tell anyone else about what made Mehron collapse, because they wouldn't have believed me." She paused, searching his face for reassurance. He waited. "During one of my visions, I came back with something from the past. It was part of a wooden sign with some sort of scroll on it that certified the land belonged to the Mi'kmaq people. I had it on my desk. Mehron asked what it was and picked it up and—she just—it was, like, electrocuting her. She held it for at most three seconds, then let it go and dropped to the floor. She knocked her head on the corner of the desk, but that isn't why she's out. They can't explain it. And there's rumors about me…" Dulci's breath hitched. People were imagining that she had sent her best friend into a coma! She squeaked the next time she opened her mouth. Finn finally broke in, sliding in next to her on the bench and putting his arm around her, his mouth coming close to her ear.

"That's cuz no one knows what's going on, and they don't know *you*," he said. "If they did, they wouldn't think you could hurt a fly."

By then Dulci had screwed her face into a scowl and the hiccups had started. "But I *would*. If I could—*hiccup*—

go back to kill your ancestor, I might! I don't—*hiccup*—understand why he did it, but he kills this—*hiccup*—this innocent young girl who was just trying—*hiccup*—she was just trying to be nice to him—"

Finn's hand on her back was moving in slow circles. His near hand felt for hers, took it from where it clenched her other hand between her knees, and gently loosened it to cradle it gently.

"It's going to be okay," he said. "Now tell me from the beginning."

Chapter 22

* * *

Finn retained an admirable neutrality of expression throughout her recital, but after a few minutes of quiet, she accepted that he needed time to absorb it alone. If he did in fact believe her, he'd have some emotions come running, no doubt about that.

She left him at school with a promise to talk again soon and boarded the bus for home. The din around her was a distant hum. A silent cloud engulfed her again, allowing her to sort through the words she'd heard that day: Mr. McKenna's surprising knowledge, Finn's unexpected trust, and the vision itself, with her first view of Taytere. What to think? Where to go?

When she got home, she tossed her bag on the mudroom floor and called out for her mom and dad. Her dad was missing from his computer desk for once but her mom poked her head around the door to her office at the front of the house. She drove Dulci up to the hospital and they visited Mehron for a half-hour. Joan was there. She met Dulci's eyes briefly, then went back to watching her daughter's face, covered with tubes and tape.

Olive stayed out in the hallway, rustling through a stack of stapled papers.

When Dulci rejoined her, she nodded. They made the

return trip in the car in silence.

* * *

There was no word from Finn on her mobile phone that night, and when she passed him in the halls the next day at school, zombie though she was, she still noticed his brief, piercing look before he turned away. So he needed more time. *But does Mehron have it?* Dulci wondered.

The next day at dinner time, while her parents tried to talk of other matters in the world—Don's next sea voyage, a new grant for the town's historical society, Olive's mother's upcoming visit for Thanksgiving—Dulci managed only vague noises. She was thinking of the piece of the puzzle she'd gotten, and straining her ears to hear the chirp of her phone that would signal a text from Finn.

When they saw her go for her phone, they exhaled together. "At least it's about a boy," she heard her mother say before reaching the top of the stairs. *It's not*, she thought. *It's about a girl.*

can I come see mehron with u? i think im ready
I'm allowed to go for 1/2 hr after school, she tapped. *Tmw?*
Meet u in pkg lot

She went back downstairs to let her mom know of the change in plans, then retreated to her room. *Her piece of the puzzle.* What was she not seeing? What was Jesse seeing, that made him silent?

* * *

Thursday dawned dark grey and broody. The first big snow of the season was predicted for the holiday weekend, making Olive worried about her mother traveling on the highways from Ottawa. It would be wet and sloppy. Dark and broody.

Dulci was up early and still in her noise-muffling bubble. When she saw the dark clouds, she shivered a bit, not with thoughts of her grandmother's drive from the capital but because it made her think of her own journey to come.

She sleepwalked through another day of school. She felt a twinge of her former life intrude when she worried about her teachers thinking she was always like this, a 'problem child.' But it faded quickly, her mind burrowing back into the cave it had made for itself. She sat out P.E. with the rest of the students today: they were in the media lab to watch a famous soccer match while Coach Johnson paused it to point out interesting plays. She watched the screen as a blur of color, her mind on the imminent meeting with Finn. They would see Mehron, and then she'd take him to Jesse.

* * *

Finn was a little late meeting her in the parking lot. She stood under cover of the alcove by the steps at 3:15, starting to wonder what had happened to him, when she saw his car pull up to the curb. She leaned over to peer through the window, then climbed in.

"What, you think someone else was driving my truck?"

"No, you're just late, which isn't like you."

The teasing expression fled. "I wanted to pick up some flowers."

Dulci glanced in the tiny back seat area and saw a wrapped parcel of lilies and daisies, all bright colors and heady fragrance. "That was nice," she said. "I didn't even think of that."

He smiled briefly and squeezed her hand. "I'll be going slow and real careful. I had to promise your mom. She actually called our house last night to impress upon me the seriousness of the situation. No faith in my driving ability at all." The teasing was back, and Dulci sighed, settling in to her seat and buckling in. She wasn't up to his levity. "She got my mom, thank goodness. Dad's a bit down at the moment."

Dulci took in this news, remembering how Finn had described his dad's problems on their first date. *So he's dealing with his own shit*, she thought. *Good. I'm not the only one then.*

They got to the hospital a few minutes after four, and Joan was out in the lobby, getting some water from the drinking fountain. When she saw them, her face relaxed a little. Dulci went to give her a hug, and she hung on a long time, but Dulci didn't mind. It seemed to buoy her up as well.

"I was beginning to think you couldn't come today," she said.

"Just slower because of the roads," she said. "And Finn brought me today. Finn, this is Mrs. Tebnek, Mehron's mom."

Finn put his hand out, ready with an automatic smile to say, 'Nice to meet you,' but his expression changed before he could utter a word. Joan half-choked, spluttered, and turned away to cough really hard several times. Dulci put her hand on her back and steered the cup of water closer to her mouth.

"Here." Joan was still bent over and turned away, but Dulci crouched with her. Her breath was shallow and raspy.

"He's here to help," she reassured her. Joan placed one hand on Dulci's arm and coughed again, steadying herself. She took another long sip of the water, then turned back.

She had her left hand on her heart, her breathing again under control, as she reached out her right to greet him. "Hello, Finn MacDonald."

Dulci observed him to see if he'd take offense at Joan's reaction. But she needn't have worried; he smiled and seemed as normal as ever. *Why can't I do that? I'm sure he felt it.*

They followed Joan into the hospital room, where Mehron lay as inert as ever and covered with equipment. Dulci went to a seat to one side of the hospital bed, while Joan took the other. Finn stood next to Dulci, watching, waiting.

When Dulci had come before, she'd just sat for the thirty minutes, thinking, or praying, or whatever one wanted to call her desperate longing to see Mehron laugh at her again. She'd sat and held her hand, or patted her shin. Finn stood with his hands clasped behind him, looking down at the sight for the first time. Dulci looked again with his eyes.

Bandages, needles, bags of fluid, beeping machines, tubes: there wasn't much of Mehron to actually see. Her strong features were slack, her skin faded and splotchy. Only her hair remained as black and silky as usual. Obviously Joan had been combing it. Finn stepped a little closer, laid a hand gently on the shiny mass stretching out behind the head of the bed. He followed it up and back lightly with the back of his fingers.

Joan stuttered out a sigh. Dulci's gaze swung around to Mehron's face, half-hoping for a change, but there was nothing. She let out the breath she was holding, and laid her hand on Mehron's blanketed shin, that she might sense some warmth wherever she was.

After their time ran out, and visiting hours were over, Dulci walked with Finn out to the glass doors of the hospital entrance. It was blowing hard, and the snow was starting to pile up. A snowplow passed by on the road below, and its headlights were on high. Sunset, coming early in the storm. She turned to Finn.

"I wanted to ask you to come with me to see Jesse, but I don't think now is a good time."

"No, I wouldn't want to go down that direction tonight, even going slow. I'll take you tomorrow though."

"Instead of the hospital?"

"Yeah."

"Okay. Good."

Chapter 23

* * *

Out of soccer videos, Coach Johnson let them play Heads-up, Seven-up for a while before starting a game of his own invention: a cross between sports trivia and *Jeopardy!* Dulci sat with her head down on her knees, not looking up at the whiteboard in the borrowed classroom. When she looked up it was to sneak a glance outside, where it was grimy and slushy. They hadn't even gotten a day of pure white; it was straight to the sleety grossness of a midwinter hump day.

She chewed on another nail, wishing the bell would ring so she could get Finn down to the Mi'kmaq village and see what happened. If Jesse had had such a reaction when she'd talked about Finn, what would he do with him in the room? She didn't want him to act out the violence he'd been meditating, but she did want some pieces of the puzzle to fall together, and for that to happen, they all had to be out in the open.

Finally the bell rang; her wish was granted. She headed out to the parking lot for the second day in a row, standing just outside the big double doors. This time, Finn was at the curb at 3:03. The cab of his truck was clean as usual, and Dulci got in, pulling the door shut tight and dropping her bag on the floor between her feet.

She looked ahead. They didn't move. She turned to take in Finn, and noticed something was different. She hadn't seen it through the window, but he'd gotten a haircut, and something else…

He was looking at her too. "Dulci. Before we get to the waterfront, can you tell me a bit more about the piece of wood that you brought back?"

She focused on his words instead of the thing in his appearance that had jarred her. "Um, yeah. It's a sign that has writing on it that says the land around it belongs to the Mi'kmaq according to some royal warrant or decree, something like that."

"Did you read it?"

"Read it?"

"Yeah, how do you know that's what it said? Is some of the writing on the piece—"

"Yeah, there's writing on the piece I brought back, but it's only partial." How did she know? It had flashed on her all of a sudden when she'd gone back, but she hadn't read the whole sign, just seen a snatch of it, and then Angus's action had confirmed her hunch as true. She shrugged. "I'm not sure."

Finn pulled the truck into gear, but paused before hitting the gas. "What do you think would happen if I touched it?"

"Don't!" A flood of panic came over Dulci; she envisioned him climbing through her window and stealing the wood from its shoebox.

"Hey!" He put one hand up. "I'm just wondering, thinking aloud. Why was Mehron hurt, but you weren't? Where would I fit in, in that scale? Too close to the action? Too far?"

Dulci's heart fell from her throat back into her chest and she pushed back her shoulders. "I don't know. But I don't think it's important. I think it's important that you see Jesse. That's where the sparks are."

Finn gave her a level look, then shook his head and

pulled out. "Okay. As long as you're sure he won't haul off and kill me." An uneasy trickle of sweat down Dulci's shoulder blades acknowledged her own fear of something happening.

"I'll see how he is first. Then if it's okay, you'll come in the house. Okay?"

"Fine."

* * *

This time, Joan wasn't there to answer the door. Tuotu did, surprised to find Dulci there. Possibly Don had told him about her staying away from Jesse. Possibly not. His face was strained and looked like a cigar-store Indian, all deep creases and erect fortitude. The difference between his normal smile and this haggard caricature scared Dulci.

He looked behind her to the green truck with the engine running, but didn't voice any questions. He stepped backward and let her in. She stepped to the side in the low-lit hallway to speak with him quietly. "I came to talk to Jesse. How's he doing today?"

Tuotu's slow sigh was an answer in itself. It echoed Joan's words: *not both of them.* "He's no longer catatonic. We've got soup and bread into him and kept him warm in bed. Other than that, I think it depends on Mehron's condition." The large man shrugged at his unscientific opinion. "It's out of our hands, that much I believe."

Dulci heard the defeat in his words. Also, the acknowledgement that Dulci was involved. This family, which she loved as her own, had had so much trouble. She turned and gave him a hard hug, which he accepted with a soft hand on her shoulder. After a moment she drew back and looked at him, trying to communicate all she could not put into words. His gaze dropped and he waved her down the hall to Jesse's room.

She found him in bed, on his side with the covers pulled up to his chin. His eyes were open, and they swept to Dulci as soon as she opened the door and stood in the light from the overhead lamp. His eyes were empty, and they showed no recognition at first. Then Dulci took a step closer. She could see the sweat standing out on his temple and upper lip. She stepped quickly forward to his side. "Jesse, are you okay?"

"They took me back off the medication, but it's doing something weird to my temperature. I'm freezing when I'm not under the covers, but when I am, I burn up. Can you pass me the water, please?"

Dulci did as he asked, wondering at his placid, natural tone. Had he lost his memory? "Jesse, do you know what's happened?"

He looked back at her, gulping the water down as his eye considered her. At last he tipped the bottle back upright and let out a gasp. "They didn't tell me. But I know she's gone."

"Gone? She's not *gone*, Jesse. She's—just—stuck. She's sick, and stuck in limbo. But I think we can help her, if we all put our pieces of the puzzle together."

Jesse's eyes sharpened and the look of defeat left them a little. "What do you mean?"

"The music teacher told me we all—we time travelers —only get a piece of the puzzle, which is why we have to work together to solve the puzzle." She paused. "And I think we need Finn."

Jesse's skin, usually tan and healthy, was pale and still beaded with sweat. He clenched his jaw and looked at her. "Has he seen anything?"

"No."

"Then what possible use can he be?" he exploded. "He's the problem, not the solution, Dulci, not the way to get Mehron back!"

"But I'm the link between you and him," she said in a small voice. "He's the reason I'm seeing what I'm seeing; that's what your mom said. I think he has to help us with Kukuwi."

Jesse's face contracted in anger. He slammed the

water bottle down on the floor, flopped on his back, working his jaw and staring at the ceiling. "He's the problem. I can't—I can't see him, not while Mehron is gone. I might—" He grimaced in a terrible echo of a smile. Tears leaked out and down into the pillow as he struggled to see it how she did. He took a deep breath and lurched up into a sitting position, gathering the comforter and blankets around him like a cloak and moving to sit up against the wall side of his bed. He nodded at Dulci. She read the resolve and fear in his eyes and her heart ached for him. She turned and ran through the hallway, opened the front door and looked for the pickup.

It was no longer idling. It was parked in front of the house. There was no sidewalk, so it was a small distance from the lawn where he'd chosen to park. Finn was looking straight out the windshield, to the south. Dulci glanced in that direction, but saw nothing. When she looked back, he was watching her. Had she imagined it? He got out and came round to the door.

"Come on in," she said, holding the door open.

He caught it before it could slam, clicked it closed softly, and followed Dulci's floating figure in front of him. They arrived at the door to Jesse's bedroom and Dulci turned to look at Finn before turning the knob. She tried to show the same resolve in her look, passing on strength to Finn, as Jesse had to her. Then she opened the door.

Jesse was still enthroned in his covers on the bed, sitting straight up against the wall, facing them as they came in. Dulci wondered what Finn could be thinking at this point. He'd heard that Jesse was mentally unstable, he'd listened to Dulci's tale of visions that tied in with Jesse's, and he'd seen Mehron in a coma for no reason that the doctors could figure out. She hoped he had an open enough mind to absorb it all.

After a still moment, when nobody moved but there seemed to be an iceberg to melt in the middle of the room, Finn spoke. "Hi, Jesse. It's good to finally meet you. And I'm sorry about your sister." He glanced briefly in Dulci's direction and she tried to emit rays of encouragement. "We went to see her yesterday. I brought flowers." It seemed a very small thing to offer, especially knowing what Jesse knew of past errors. "I'm really sorry."

So he decided to go with apologizing, thought Dulci. That's good. *Now if Jesse will just remain calm...*

"What are you going to do?"

"Do?" Finn echoed.

"To bring her back. Dulci says you're part of the puzzle somehow, but you haven't *seen* anything. Haven't seen what your ancestor did, that has cursed this family for generations. If only we had the power to—" his fierce mask broke for a second and he drew a shaky breath. The mask fell back into place. "But we don't have the ability to fix this. So *you* have to be the one. No?"

"I don't—I don't know what you mean. Dulci said you think that some MacDonald was the one that gave that Indian girl a stab wound."

"He did! Taytere says so!"

"What else did he say?"

"He said that she was being disloyal, she was being too kind to the enemy, and that's how she was lured in. Killed! A ten-year-old girl! Like my sister, when I first started—"

Jesse choked off the rest of the sentence, turning his glare to Dulci. She saw he was shaking. His eyes rounded, dimmed, as he looked at her. The fire went out of him in a slump and he leaned over to cough.

Dulci went toward the bedside table, grabbing the next water bottle and uncapping it for him. "Jesse, here. Drink." She put it under his head and he grabbed it. She put her hand on his back, aching to tell him it would be okay, but knowing she could not. *Oh, for the days of believing in parents' all-mighty powers,* she thought. A prickle of sensation went up her own spine. She shivered, and caught Finn's glance at her. What was happening?

She felt the hairs at the base of her neck sing with electricity. Was she going back, now, alone? She grabbed for Jesse's hand and the bedstead knob, feeling the blast of cold, as if it was under her skin instead of in the air.

Her eyes met Jesse's, veiled with acceptance. She turned to look for Finn five feet away. He was standing tall and stock-still, staring with horror at the middle of the room, where a cloud of silver fog was swirling. A voice spoke in Dulci's head.

"Take it. Take them. Find me. I won't know yet…"

A clatter, as something fell from the cloud. A small drum, not unlike her bodhràn, but an earlier, more rustic design. The animal skin not machine-cleaned, a tipper made of real bone attached by a leather thong to the drum's wooden rim. She hopped down to pick it up. "Did you hear that?" she asked Finn, in a voice that competed with something whirling, a wind picking up inside the room.

He shook his head. She whipped her head back to Jesse. "Did you hear her?"

Jesse raised his eyes, shook his head too. She was the driver, then. She grabbed Finn by the elbow and pulled him over to sit on the edge of the bed. She raised the drum as she scrambled up onto the mattress between the two of them. The wind took her out of herself. No more numbness. She called on any kind spirits for their help. She felt, rather than saw, Kukuwi's sly smile as she had first seen it in that vision on the soccer field, when she'd asked for help, with Angus and her family. She closed her eyes and started drumming fast right away. She got through eight beats, then she no longer felt the thing in her hands.

Chapter 24

* * *

She was standing in snow again. As the eerie vision of wind and fog in Jesse's room left her, she felt the cold. The stars looked down upon a field of pure white snow. She looked around, wondering where Jesse and Finn had got to. *They should be here. They have to be here.*

She saw a hill rising to her left. *I'll make for that and see if I can see them anywhere close.* She took her first trudging steps, lamenting that she hadn't put snow shoes on to visit Jesse. At least she had thick wool socks on, and her rain boots. Those would help for a while. *How long will I be here?* she wondered. *Until I get it right? That could be forever.* As soon as the flippant expression formed itself in her mind, she tried to put it out. *No, I will be going home soon. Right after we rescue Mehron.* But where was the rest of the 'we'?

* * *

Jesse knelt in snow, heaving great breaths of air, still clutching a quilt and several blankets around him. He had no shoes on, just the cotton slipper-socks he'd gotten from his mom last Christmas. Purple. *Ridiculous*, his mind murmured to him as he tried to measure his breathing. The hill looked familiar: white spruce and yellow birch surrounding him on the low ground below. He had a good view of the surrounding country from where he was, even though it was only moonlight and starlight. He saw a figure struggling to lift its feet high enough to wade through the snow, coming in his direction.

He wondered if he should, then called out down the slope. "Dulci!"

The figure stopped and looked up. He moved up so that he formed a better silhouette against the dark sky. She waved, and altered course slightly to climb up to him. He felt immense relief. *Not alone this time.* Quickly followed by fear. *What would happen to her here?*

* * *

Dulci struggled as fast as she could to climb the hillside. It still took a good five minutes to come up to where she'd seen him, fifty feet above the little valley. *Where was Finn?* She worried about one thing while working towards the other. When she reached the top, she felt whatever food was in her belly quake and roll over. At least the two of them were there, together. "Do you see Finn?"

"No."

Dulci eyed him. Was he lying? They really couldn't afford that now, here. "You're sure?"

His voice was quieter when he said yes, and she remembered the face of resolve and fear. She took his hand and folded her fingers into it. Squeezed. She kept it there as she scanned the horizon in all directions looking for movement. Finally, along the ridge she saw something. It was a small dark shape. *Rabbit? No...*

It had to be Kukuwi. Dulci knew when she stopped and the wind picked up her hair to play with it. It was the same long black hair that she remembered from that day on the soccer field, in the ditch...

It was that night. It was going to happen. She tightened her grip on Jesse's hand and found him narrowing his eyes at the small figure. Then they widened again, and their eyes met. *He knows it too.*

"So what are we going to do, wait for Angus to appear and all gang up on him? He could still beat us. We didn't take any weapons."

"We won't need weapons," Dulci said, watching as Kukuwi made her way across the ridge to them.

She stopped about ten feet away, cocked her head. *She speaks English now*, Dulci reminded herself. That recalled Taytere, who had spoken French instead. *Where was he now? He could come in handy…*

"I know you," she said to Jesse. She smiled. He smiled back, a twist of hope making it bittersweet.

"I remember you," she said to Dulci. She hesitated. "I ask for your help with land and my family. Is this answer? The tribe to leave and white man to live?"

She was describing what had happened, Dulci realized: how Angus had conspired with authorities to steal the land meant for tribal use. Apparently, at least some of the tribe members had decided to leave after the incident. Dulci wanted to lift her shoulders in an I-don't-know gesture, but that might not be understood, and if she was going to be the spirit guide Kukuwi thought she was, shrugging was out of the question.

"It has to be," she said simply. Kukuwi acknowledged the answer with a sigh. "But you are in danger, Kukuwi."

"I am —?" She didn't understand.

"In danger," Jesse supplied. He said a word in Mi'kmaq that Dulci didn't recognize, and Kukuwi looked back at her, the question in her eyes.

"From Angus MacDonald," Jesse continued. This time Kukuwi cocked her head again, perplexed and doubtful. Before she could ask anything, movement from behind Jesse and Dulci caught her attention and she tensed. They turned to look, scampering closer together, and saw a larger form coming along from the other side of the ridge. *Something familiar…*

"Finn!" Dulci said in the largest stage whisper ever. The figure looked up from fifty yards away, raised an arm, and kept coming. Jesse hmphed, and Kukuwi looked worried. "Who is he?"

"Young man," Jesse grunted. "My age. But white."

"His name is Finn MacDonald," Dulci said, an edge to her tone for Jesse's benefit. He didn't look over.

"Mac-Do-nal," she sounded. "Angus family?"

"Yes," Dulci and Jesse both said.

Finn reached them at last, there was a rough introduction, and then they all four stood staring at each other in a shadowy moonlit circle. Finn spoke first.

"What are you doing out here?" He hadn't been awed by the jolt of recognition of The Night of The Murder that she and Jesse had. Of course he wouldn't have.

"I wait for you, and you." She pointed at Dulci and Jesse. "My spirits. I learn Angus change law tonight. I no sure what I should think."

"Change the law… you mean with the sign and then with the government?" Dulci asked. She nodded. Her gaze slid over to Finn.

"You sure are Angus family," she said, and pointed to his hair and eyes, and lastly, to his mouth. "Same. Kind."

Finn smiled, getting bashful with what sounded like a compliment. Jesse spoke again, in Mi'kmaq. Kukuwi's delighted expression changed to one of apprehension. *He's reminding her she's in danger,* Dulci thought. *From the white man, no doubt.* She scanned the horizon again, and saw no reddish-gold glint in the moonlight. She looked back at Finn's hair and hoped they could talk Angus out of whatever reason he had for stabbing this girl, who obviously considered him to be like a father. *I wish I knew more of the story,* Dulci thought. She hated having to act without knowing all the information. But Mehron was back home laid low by the power of this curse, so she had to jump at this chance.

They were murmuring, low voices in conversation, when Jesse's ear picked up something dissonant in the snowy night. They all saw him move, then stopped their chatter and faced out to the night, straining to see what he'd detected. It was a tapping noise, two hard things knocking together, which was unusual amid all the snow. No one made a sound, and gradually they all heard it. Like finger-bones on a necklace knocking together…

Finn pointed a finger and they all turned to look in the direction he pointed. A figure was drawing closer, all right, but who was it? *Why was everyone and their mother up and about tonight?* About forty feet away, they could discern details: long black hair, big fur cloak, man's height.

The next sound was easy to identify for three of the waiting pairs of ears: the sound of a long knife being withdrawn from a steel sheath.

"NO!" the cry came from Dulci's elbow and she nearly fell over on her side, it surprised her so much. Jesse had his arms outstretched toward the coming figure, but whether it was to block his view or to grab hold of him, she couldn't tell. Jesse's face held no more fear, nor resolve, only despair. Dulci looked back to the figure.

It was Taytere.

Chapter 25

* * *

"Fucking, lying, sonofabitch!" Jesse's voice started low and ended in a shout. He'd sunk down into the snow. Tears started down his face, glinting in the moonlight. Dulci looked back to the figure, still advancing slowly. She saw it in a flash.

Finn looked confused, worried about why Jesse was freaking out, and ignorant of who was coming. Kukuwi was not. She'd seen him, heard him, and stepped over to Dulci, positioning herself slightly behind everyone.

"It was Taytere." Dulci said it softly, and Finn looked over. "It *is* Taytere."

His look of confusion deepened. "But why—"

"My brother no like me stay with Angus," Kukuwi whispered. "And my tribe, everyone no like Angus change law."

So her tribe thought she'd sided with Angus in the land dispute. And Angus had only been trying to protect her from her brother... his voice from that other starry night came back to her: "*I am protecting my new daughter.*" But then where had that first vision come from? Angus wandering around crying with a knife... *oh no.* He was crying for *Kukuwi's* death this night, not for his dead wife and child, long since gone and buried. The images slid into slots now. But what had Jesse seen that had convinced him that Angus had killed Kukuwi?

Taytere was only thirty feet away, and within hearing distance. He had stopped, perhaps expecting to find one instead of four.

"You told me it was the Scot's fault! How could you lie—to *me*?" This was Jesse. He put all his sense of betrayal into those final two words. But if Taytere understood, he didn't show it. He stood stock-still. Did he not understand English yet? Dulci translated for him.

"Vous lui avez dit que c'etait la faute de l'Ecossais. Comment vous pouviez lui trahi comme ca?"

She'd used the word for "betray," instead of "lie," since that was the intense feeling she was getting from Jesse, overriding even her own vocabulary. Taytere's head swiveled in her direction. "Mais j'ai personne trahi, Demoiselle. C'est *elle* qui *nous* a trahi." He pointed an accusing finger at his young sister. She didn't understand the French, but she knew her brother was laying blame at her feet. Dulci saw her set her quivering chin and her eyes blaze in defiance. Dulci was glad; maybe they had come at the right moment this time.

Jesse had understood his accusation of betrayal as well. He staggered to stand again, putting a hand on Finn's shoulder for support. He called out a few things in Mi'kmaq. Kukuwi straightened up. Taytere looked daggers at him, then switched his gaze to Finn. "Et qui est-ce, cet homme?"

He was replying to her in French instead of answering Jesse's question in Mi'kmaq; what did that signify? "C'est un ami," she said: *a friend*.

"Un ami Ecossais?" *A Scottish friend?*

It was pointless to deny it. His height, his coloring, the way he carried himself, he could have been a Scotsman just off the boat. Taytere probably knew that he was related to Angus as well. That meant he was in immediate danger, just like Kukuwi. Because while Taytere might hesitate to kill a grown man known in his village, he would not be afraid of attacking a boy his age that no one knew of or would be looking for.

But Jesse stood in front of him. She didn't know how much Finn was following. He'd been terrible at his French flash cards, but she thought he could probably follow the simple conversation. Jesse, though, was following Taytere's expression, which had become wolf-like. His lower jaw thrust forward, his nostrils flared.

There they stood, little Dulci in front of littler Kukuwi, wiry Jesse in front of hockey-player Finn. Taytere kept his long knife out, but wavered. What could he do that would not lose face? *He's wondering if he should attack us anyway, and die in glorious battle*, Dulci thought, and didn't like it one bit. Like Jesse said, they hadn't brought weapons, and he could very likely overcome them all if he chose. But he didn't know that.

Dulci made her move. "Et si je vous ai dit que l'Ecossais quittera, que diriez-vous?" *What if I told you that the Scot would leave.*

"Pour toujours?" *Forever?*

"Oui."

"Ça m'arrangerait." *That would suit me fine.*

"Et si je vous ai dit que votre soeur lui suivrait?" *And if I told you that your sister would follow him?*

His face darkened, his gaze flicking back and forth among the various faces, all inspiring a different form of hate except Jesse's. Dulci turned to Jesse, whose face still registered pain at the betrayal of his vision-ancestor, and loathing.

"What did you ask him?" Dulci asked him, sotto voce.

"I said," he paused. "She is still his sister. And that I would do anything to heal my sister, lying sick right now because of his deed, what he is going to do."

Dulci caught her breath, turning to look at Taytere again. *He had not answered Jesse. Was that his sore spot? What would get him to leave them alone and not cause the curse?* The curse!

"Si vous tuez votre soeur, toute votre famille sera maudite, même en trois cent années. Vous les maudissez avec cette action." If a curse that followed his family for three hundred years was not enough of a deterrent, what was?

"Maudit? Vous ne vous rendez pas compte que nous sommes déjà maudits, avec ces hommes?" He waved his knife over in Finn's direction. Dulci didn't answer his cynical statement, calling the white immigrants the curse of his own time.

A look of suspicion came into Taytere's eyes then. Perhaps he was figuring out who they were, spirits from the future, and that it was useless to fight against them. Dulci hoped so. His eyes shifted to Jesse's, and a fraction of relaxation came into his stance.

Jesse was still leaning forward in a ferocious posture, angry and ready to defend. Taytere spoke to him then, and Dulci could only follow the body language. Taytere pointed once more with the knife, this time toward Kukuwi, then sheathed it. He spoke. Jesse answered. The iron went out of Taytere's spine. He met Jesse's gaze straight on, spoke again. Jesse straightened, gave a barely perceptible nod.

"What's happening?" Finn said out of the side of his mouth to Dulci. With the French and the Mi'kmaq and the backstory he hadn't witnessed, Dulci realized he must be completely lost.

"I'm not sure. Either Jesse's guilting him into going away, or explaining that we're…spirits." It sounded odd to say out loud, but that was how she'd been thinking of herself in this time, for what would they call someone from here coming to 2013? A ghost? She liked spirit better.

Finn kept his gaze on Taytere; they all did. After another moment where he surveyed them frankly—was it getting lighter?—he spoke to his sister in their language.

Jesse's eyes flashed, but he did not move toward him. Apparently he hadn't forgiven Kukuwi, just decided she wasn't worth torturing the family forever over. *What a brother.*

He turned to go, then turned back, and gave a sort of salute to Jesse. Then he turned to Finn, his eyes skimming over his familiar features, dismissing him. And finally he looked on Dulci. "A la prochaine," he said, with the barest hint of a smile. They watched him walk away for several long minutes, until he'd descended the ridge and gone through the trees toward the sea. It was definitely getting lighter. A royal blue shone through the inky black in patches, indicating where the world turned toward the light.

Dulci faced Kukuwi slowly. "You know you must go away from here?"

"Yes. I see now. That is our answer. Thank you."

She responded graciously to spirits from another age, for a ten-year-old. What could Dulci give her that would give her courage for the long road ahead? "Thank *you*," she replied. "You came to us, you know, to help Angus and—" She looked over at Jesse. "—to help us. It was very brave. I almost didn't do it myself." She smiled, and was rewarded with an answering smile. "Now go find Angus and tell him we wish him well on his journey. Make it a good story." Kukuwi took her hand in both of hers and kissed it. She looked at the two young men, comparing them somehow. With a final glance at Dulci, and that same form of salute her brother had given, she walked off in the opposite direction.

Did she feel any different? Did Jesse? She turned to ask him and saw that both he and Finn gazed down the slope of the hill to the sea. She looked down, and saw the beginnings of a late dawn, for it was October and winter approaching.

"Want to go see the sunrise?" Finn asked.

"Yes," Jesse replied, his eyes already transfixed by the

sight.

"Sure," Dulci said, and started down carefully.

The clouds were just starting to show tinges of purple as they reached the shore. It was rocky, with big black rocks sharing space with thousands of grey and white pebbles. They found a promontory, a big rock where people might have sat to watch the sea for generations.

Finn stepped up on it first, and vanished. Dulci's shoulders tightened; her spine tingled. Jesse turned and gave her a look. He dashed back to where she was and grabbed her in a hug. "It's gone," he said into her hair. "Even here, I can tell." He pulled back, and touched his chest with his middle finger. "Gone." A light entered his face that had not been there. Instead of a thank you, which Dulci expected was coming, he lowered his lips to hers. Dulci felt the warm air from his nose, the urgency in his mouth, the energy in his arms. Her surprised hands eventually came down to settle on his back. She melted into the kiss, absorbing all the trailing energy from their final encounter, and losing herself in it. She felt her heart beating, then heard another beat. Was it Jesse's? It quickened and she realized it was the drum, once again in her hands.

Chapter 26

* * *

Dulci pulled back to open her eyes, seeing that she now sat on the lawn outside the Tebneks' house, holding the old drum. Her lips tingled.

It looked like late afternoon, not long after the time they'd 'left.' Where were the others?

She moved her legs and found them to be sore. Her head ached also as soon as she moved her neck. *Ow.* She staggered to stand and dusted her backside of all the leaf-dust and grime. She slipped the antique drum into the large inside pocket of her jacket and made her way to the front door again. She knocked. Looking around at the street and seeing no one, she decided to go in, but just then the green truck caught her eye. Something pinged in her memory. *Finn.* Before going in, she would check his truck.

She went back down the slope of the lawn and peered into the truck. Through its dusty windows she could see a form halfway in the driver's footwell and half on the seat. She opened the door and leaned over the passenger side. His head was turned away from her on the seat. "Finn," she said, nudging his shoulder.

"Wha—" he said sleepily, jerking his head up and hitting it directly on the steering wheel. "Ow!"

"Sorry," she said.

"Wha' happened? Why am I all scrunched up in here?" A cold stone dropped in Dulci's stomach.

"Don't you remember?"

"Remember what? You dragging me here to talk to Jesse? I *drove* you here. Obviously." His sarcasm switched to grudging puzzlement. "I don't remember how I got under here, though." He opened the driver's side door enough to get a leg out and weasel out from under the steering column. "Ouch, that fucking—I mean, that really hurts," he finished, looking sheepishly at Dulci across the cab of the truck. He rubbed his head. "Massive headache," he said.

Dulci wondered if Jesse would also be cursing when he woke up. *OK, time to get back in the house.* "I'm going in," she said.

"Hey, wait! I said I'd come—just let me shake out the sleep."

She strode back up the grass, ignoring the pain in her own body, not bothering to knock on the door this time. Where had Tuotu gone? Hadn't he answered the door when they'd gotten there before? She walked down the hallway to Jesse's bedroom. The door was ajar.

She found Tuotu there, cradling the head of his son on the bed. Jesse lay stretched out, eyes closed, his mouth slightly open. Dulci felt her stomach go squirmy, and wondered if she was going to throw up. She looked up at Tuotu.

"He went still a bit ago," he said quietly. "I can hear his heart beat and he's breathing, but I can't wake him. I don't have the heart to call the hospital."

He breathed. His heart was beating. Dulci felt the tide of acid subside. She stepped to the bed, remembering the sight of him huddled in blankets, sitting up against the wall. She couldn't swallow past a big lump as she looked down on the luminous face, which looked so peaceful now. She traced an eyebrow lightly with her finger. "You said it's gone," she whispered. "You said you could feel it."

She had not gone through *all that* to lose Jesse. She leaned over and kissed him on the cheek. The slight coldness in his skin chilled her more than his stillness. She felt a presence in the doorway to the bedroom, and realized Finn must be there. She sighed, and her breath hitched, making it sound like she was either crying, or choking. She smiled. *Maybe Jesse would wake up and not remember anything of the last four years*, she thought. That might be a blessing, cursed as they were for him. *Except for today*. She put a hand on his chest, willing him to remember that kiss. She felt the heartbeat, and even imagined she felt it getting stronger. Her fingers recalled the beats of the old drum going full force, taking them from that snowy night that she would never forget. She envisioned the heart of the drum going into Jesse's chest, healing him. Then she stepped away.

I should call Joan at the hospital, see if there's a change in Mehron, she thought. *There goddam-well-better-be*. She looked up at Finn, whose brow was quirked in confusion. Again. *But at least he was being quiet, understanding the gravity of the—*

"Dulci?"

Her head back whipped around and she stepped quickly back to the bed. Tuotu was brushing back the hair from Jesse's face. His eyes were open, but he wasn't moving right away. Her hand went to hold one of his. "Right here. How are you feeling?"

He looked at her, his eyes probing. "Like I went to hell and back."

She gave his fingers a tiny squeeze. "Was I there?"

"Yeah. And so was that bastard," he said, his eyes flicking toward Finn. Dulci let out her breath. *He remembered.*

Tuotu maneuvered behind to help him sit up, Jesse grimacing the whole time. His eyes found Dulci again, and she blushed. She groped for something to say. "I ended up on your lawn. And Finn ended up stuffed in his car, under the steering wheel. Headache?" A slight nod, another grimace.

"What did you guys do?" Tuotu asked. "Or do I want to know?"

"You do, sir, if you want to know why Mehron will get better." Jesse's weak voice contrasted with his knowing smirk.

"How—how do you know? What are you talking about?" Tuotu's voice was hopeful.

"Just call the hospital, Dad. It's gone."

"What's—never mind. Lemme get the phone." He gingerly let go of his son, then hurried out of the room. Dulci felt her face still red, but calming down. "Finn doesn't remember," she murmured to Jesse as he adjusted how he was sitting, scooting to the edge of the bed. She wasn't sure he'd heard her until a moment later he glanced at Finn and asked, "So how'd you end up under your steering column?" with the open face and offhand manner of a country hick asking where the pigs had got to.

Finn shifted his feet. "I don't exactly know, unless Dulci…"

She shook her head. "Don't even try to blame it on me. I just woke you up."

"But I did drive you here? To have a conversation? I'm not going crazy?"

Jesse and she shared a look, almost a giggle. "No, you're not. We had the conversation. You just don't remember it. That's okay."

"It's better than okay," Jesse said. "Because I am no longer crazy either. In fact, I might even go back to high school with you guys."

"No, that would make you crazy all over again. No one wants to be in high school," Dulci said.

"Well, they might if it was where you were." A stunned silence. Jesse had gone ahead and leapt into the chasm. Right in front of Finn. What could she say? She turned to Finn, her mouth open to spin tales of placation, but saw that he was looking at her strangely. Rather as if he was trying to remember something. Maybe why he was attracted to her in the first place. She felt a little puff of vanity dying inside, but smiled at him. A friendly smile.

Tuotu came back in, the cordless phone still in his hand. "She's awake," he said, stunned and joyous and mystified.

"Let's all go up St. Ann's!" Dulci said.

"Do we have a car that will fit us all?"

"Yeah, we're bringing Mom and Mehron back, remember."

"Ahh, two cars then. I'll take the Ford and meet you there?" Tuotu asked Finn.

"I'll come with you, Dad." Jesse said, moving awkwardly off the bed and attempting to stretch his obviously sore back. After several rounds of assurances that he was okay, they split up, two and two, to drive to the hospital. Dulci had plenty of time in the silence with Finn to wonder how Jesse was going to bounce back from the last four years. She figured that Taytere had been appearing and appealing to him to avenge his sister, without telling him that it wasn't her death he would be avenging, but her fateful decision to befriend Angus. She wondered if Taytere's ghost was motivated not only by rage but by guilt, as he had been the one to kill his sister. And to finally have it come to this conclusion because of Finn's return… she hoped it was a happy reunion at the hospital, and that both Jesse and Mehron bounced back easily from their brush with the past.

Joan was waiting for the party when they knocked on the door of the private room, and after throwing her arms around Tuotu, first through the door, she burst upon Dulci next. She hugged and rocked her from side to side, and Dulci hung on to comfort her. Mehron was back; she caught glimpses every time she was rocked to the right, of a grinning face, no longer connected to tubes or IVs or noisy machines. Finally, Joan pulled back, her eyes shiny with happy tears. She glanced over to the others who'd followed Dulci in, and was promptly shocked into fresh tears as she saw her son smiling, his face free of storm clouds. Jesse stepped forward and held out his arms to envelop her in a hug of his own. She was hiccuping now with emotion, and both Dulci and Finn stepped back from the family circle.

Dulci edged around to where Mehron was sitting up against many insubstantial hospital pillows. She wasn't sure how to approach her. She'd been angry for not being told, then resistant to hearing the truth, but now what? Mehron looked at her with the same look she gave her when she was being a doofus about studying. "Come on, Dulci. You're my best friend. It wasn't your fault."

"I know, but…what happened? Do you remember anything?"

"I remember picking up that petrified wood thing on your desk, then blacking out. I knew I was going, but couldn't stop it. Mom's been telling me—I've just been unconscious since then. Confounding the doctors. When I woke up, they all rushed in to ask questions and draw blood, but…Mom scared them all off after she got your guys' phone call." She grinned, then winced.

Her words drifted off, and Dulci understood she wanted some time with her family, especially to see how her brother was, now seemingly back from the dead. Jesse was murmuring low to Joan, his eyes trained on Dulci's. She stepped back to where Finn stood near the door, awkward and wanting to leave the family to its reunion in private. She caught his eye and waggled her eyebrows toward the exit. He waved her forward and then closed the door quietly behind them. They both let out huge exhales. Dulci spoke first.

"Can you give me a ride home? I bet it's about dinner time. You can stay over if you like. I'm sure Mom's got something good cooking away."

"Yeah, sure, I—" but he looked at her and stopped. "I don't know how to say this any nicer, Dulci, but—"

"I know."

"What d'you mean, you know?"

"You want to be just friends."

His back went from rigid and tree-like to slumped, relaxed. "Yeah. I didn't want to hurt your feelings though. I just—I don't think we're—you know."

Dulci almost rolled her eyes, but resisted. Good manners reasserting themselves. *Boys.* This whole weeks-long infatuation with Finn: Fate. But if it had helped the Tebneks, she could spare a few weeks and bear the rocky start to high school. Now, as to what her parents were going to say about her music club participation… she would fight that battle when she came to it. For now, they would go back to dinner with some very good news, and Just. Be. Normal. As soon as she thought it, Taytere's parting words drifted back into her mind: *A la prochaine.* Would she see any of them again?

Chapter 27

* * *

Once their late dinner was over, she thought she'd managed to ease her parents' fears about her highly irregular behavior enough that she might be able to spring some music club participation on them sooner rather than later. There was some lingering awkwardness when Dulci walked Finn to the front door, especially because she wondered if he'd seen the kiss she'd given Jesse before he'd 'come back.' On the cheek, but still. Thoughts of his other kiss rose to overwhelm the small one she'd given, and she blushed as she said good-bye with an awkward hug.

She went back to the kitchen, volunteering to do the dishes. Her surprised mother gave her a blank look, and her father, who'd been excavating the sponge in the sink, turned to quirk an eyebrow at her. He was onto her attempt to butter them up, but no matter. She washed the dishes in a sink full of warm water. *What are a bunch of gooey food particles compared to time travel?* she thought, trying to consider herself above the ickiness. It sort of worked. She mechanically circled each plate, automatically searching for spots, before loading them into the dishwasher. She let her mind wander in the background. *I wonder if this is how artists work,* she thought. *One task in the foreground, others running like open browsers in the background.*

A few things niggled at her sense of finality. Yes, Jesse was convinced he was 'healed,' or released of the curse of his ancestor's doings. And yes, Mehron was back to her normal, healthy self. But how had Mr. McKenna known about their situation? Was he a time traveler too? Not only that, he sounded like an expert, the casual way he'd asked her questions and prodded her on one point. She had to go back and ask him more about this whole… strange ability, and see if she was likely to continue having these kinds of experiences. If so, she'd need to get a better bearing on the travel part. Maybe she'd end up over time like Mr. McKenna himself, making nothing of it! "Oh, just popped down to the thirteenth century, my dear, to tell a few Gothic sculptors what they ought to be doing, you know…" The thought made her smile.

She pressed the ON button for their super-quiet dishwasher and after grabbing her book-bag from the mudroom, plodded up the stairs for bed. Now for the real makeup work at school, Dulci thought, her whole body sagging with the thought of a basic restart to most of the subjects she was taking. She would need help with the labs for general science, but she could start by catching up on history reading. She dug out the textbook. They had gone from New World Explorers to Old World Enlightenment, and she tried to remember all the names that would have to be matched with the ideas.

"I think, therefore I am."

"A wise man proportions his belief to the evidence."

"Men are born free, and everywhere they are in chains."

The next time her mind wandered, it showed her the picture of their little band of time rebels: Jesse, Finn, herself, and Kukuwi, all facing Taytere. She wished she could have seen Angus, but then again, he wouldn't have known the sadness she'd saved him from, and would only be lamenting the need to move and never come back to this island. Perhaps it was better this way.

The other niggling thoughts hummed around her head like interested wasps at a barbecue. What would the records show now? What would Joan think had happened now? Who kept their memories, and who started over when history changed? Who decided?

Maybe she could go to the library tomorrow and see what some of the old newspapers said now. But first, she had to see if the contents of the shoebox had changed. It had been several days since she shoved it in there, but she hadn't touched it. Angus had still torn off the sign. She had pleaded with him not to, but he had. Would it still be there?

She squatted next to the box in question with some trepidation. Surely she wouldn't be whisked off if she touched it now? Even more trepidation. She flicked off the lid with her hand quickly, and saw the same cobwebby rotting piece of wood, covered with a tough leathery substance with blackened markings and splotches. The same piece of wood. She left it as it was, putting the lid back on carefully, and making room for it to go in the very farthest corner of her crowded closet. Crawling backwards out of the darkened corner, she sat back on her heels and dusted her knees off. Dust bunnies will have to go, she thought.

As she did so, she felt something jangle in her jacket pocket. The same jacket she'd been wearing when she went back. The Indian drum. She froze for a moment, staring down at it, feeling the weight of it, which she hadn't noticed for the past hour or more at dinner and chores. She pulled it out slowly and looked from her bodhràn to the Indian version. Was this the key to traveling? It looked old, but not as decrepit as the piece of signpost in her closet. Maybe it had just been better taken care of.

She placed it carefully on the shelf beside the bodhràn. It looked good like that, she decided.

So, to the library, tomorrow. For now, back to the *other*

history books.

Chapter 28

* * *

When she woke the next morning, the library was not the first thing on her mind. She looked sideways, saw the blinking light that meant messages on her phone and grabbed it off the nightstand. She brought up the messaging screen. It was from Mehron. It read:

I owe you a lot. Let's meet Tue after school to talk. K?

That's weird, Dulci thought. *Doesn't sound like her. I wonder if she's feeling some after-effects of the coma. I mean, she does owe me, but she would've done the same for me, I know.* But she shrugged it off, planning on inviting her along to the library, if she was up to it. But her parents had other ideas. Her grandmother would be arriving mid-afternoon for the holiday weekend, and Dulci would be expected to stay for the visit. She would stay until Thanksgiving Monday, then head back home.

Dulci sighed for the expectations she was still required to fulfill, but the realization that she had bucked some of the others made her quietly satisfied. *I will play my Celtic music*, she thought. *I will stand by my beliefs and help my friends.* The weekend passed in a warm fuzzy haze, the heaters fogging up the windows, making the shore look like a misty enchantment. Even so, Sunday at dusk, Dulci looked out from her bedroom window and thought she saw two figures standing on the lawn, their arms up in a sort of salute. She blinked, and the shadows vanished.

* * *

It was fairly boisterous on the bus Tuesday. Everyone exclaimed over their sports games, their family visits, their holiday movies seen. Dulci kept her eyes out the window, staring at the fog over the water as the bus wound its way along the coast road.

She strained to pay attention in classes. At least she wasn't distracted by the fear of the visions coming back, but she felt so tired. Her head occasionally ached like the dickens, and she walked slowly. In her mid-quarter advisory session, her advisor asked if she thought she was up to school again. *Ah well, I guess my zombie routine didn't go unnoticed.* She said yes, and they detailed some plans to get extra time with her lab teachers after school to catch up.

By lunch time she wanted only to go home and curl up on her bed for a nap. Her brain was buzzing, her body felt brittle, and she hadn't seen a friend's face all day. She didn't blame Mehron for staying home. She stayed near the school building, venturing out only as far as the first picnic tables to eat her ham sandwich. But just a few minutes later, Mehron found her there, and flounced down to sit across from her with obvious high spirits.

"Wow, you're back to normal quick."

"Yeah," Mehron said. "Inexplicable." She looked at Dulci with a smile hovering around the corners of her mouth, then they both burst out laughing.

"I just got in. Slept late. Had to go back to the hospital twice over the weekend to discuss tests. Blah, blah, blah."

"What are the E.R. doctors going to think?"

"I dunno, but I don't wanna go back for any more testing. Did enough of that yesterday." She rolled her eyes.

"Did you have something in mind after school?"

"Like what?"

"I dunno. I was going to go to the library, but—"

"Library?! Dulci, you have to ride this wave of attention. Listen, I've gotten cards and flowers and candy from every classroom I walk into today—it's awesome!" Her eyes shone with excitement. Dulci supposed she'd be as excited if it had been happening to her. But it wasn't. No one knew that she'd had anything to do with it, other than that she was the best friend, in whose house Mehron had collapsed. She hoped there weren't any more rumors about it being a jealous rampage over Finn.

Something must have passed over her face that showed her horror at the thought, because Mehron touched her on the shoulder. "Hey. So you want to tell me what happened while I was out? I won't ask any questions till the end, and I promise I'll try to believe it." She paused and looked away down the field. "Jesse hasn't told me anything about it yet, just goes around smiling and whistling. So at least there's *that*," she said, grinning again.

"Maybe he's just getting used to being alone in his head again. I was dreading the next vision, but I wasn't always having them, like it sounded like he was."

"Maybe." Mehron opened her backpack. "Here, enjoy the fruits of your labor," she said, parceling out the chocolate hearts she'd gotten from her last class. "I do know that much, Dulci. If it hadn't been for *you* figuring it out, I'd still be half-dead." She walked around the picnic bench to Dulci's side and hugged her. Then she sat down beside her. "So." She took a deep breath. "Lay it on me."

Dulci proceeded to tell her what had happened since she'd come over and been essentially taken hostage by the Fates that wanted this wrong to be set right. She went over the hospital visits, the talk with Finn, the meeting with Jesse, the meeting in the snow, the sunrise. She left out the kiss she'd shared with Jesse, however. She'd let him move at his own pace back into the present-day world. But she really hoped he'd have time for her once he was on his own two feet. They shared a bond now that was unique to them alone. Finn had not remembered. Mehron had not been there.

When she was finished, there was a short silence, and then the bell rang. They walked back up together, the subject switching to Dulci's plan to catch up on her good grades, and Mehron's to catch up on her average ones. If anyone else was listening, they would think they were normal teenagers. Dulci let that feeling sink in for a moment.

* * *

She didn't suit up for P.E. but asked for some stretches for her legs, which she rotated through for twenty minutes, before retiring to the bench to watch the rest of the class in the gym now shooting hoops. *Soccer's done, I guess.* Four weeks of high school—was that all that had passed? And yet so much had already happened, she felt like she was ready for Christmas break. Or college.

She'd gone on several dates. She'd kissed not one, but two, boys. She'd started the music club (even if she'd had to abandon it). She'd had a really weird experience with some people from the past, but now that was over. She'd rescued her best friend from a coma, and her brother from eternal torment of the mind. All in all, a pretty good record.

When the final bell rang, she changed out the books in her locker and grabbed her big coat. She scanned the hall for Mehron as she made her way to the parking lot, where she expected to meet her. No sign. Out in the lot, students were chatting in knots. A lot of flirting among the upperclassmen, she saw. Most of the underclassmen, without a license, had to get to the bus stop out on the road or meet their parents at the front of the building. So where was Mehron? She wanted to leave fairly quickly to get in the time studying those old records.

Before too long, she saw Finn come out and head for his car. He moved without looking around, as if deep in thought. His car wasn't far from where she stood near the covered entrance, and he looked up just before climbing into the cab. He paused. Smiled hesitantly. She waved and saw his shoulders relax. He climbed in and gave her a wave through the window. She watched him drive away, strangely relieved. At least she knew now.

Ten minutes stretched to fifteen and then twenty. She'd sent Mehron a text, but the only answer had been *Have fun @library, ask if u can come 4 dinner.* She was going to give up and brave the cold to walk over alone when an old blue El Camino pulled into the parking lot entrance. It roared without even trying, and Dulci immediately knew whose it was. She ran without thinking, stopping only when her senses told her she was about to be run over by a car backing out. That obstacle dodged, she ran the rest of the way, coming up on the driver's side to lean in.

"Hey," said Jesse. "I was here all day with the guidance counselor and some of the other teachers, so I had to get out and grab something for lunch. Want some?" He picked up the bag of sandwiches from Pete's downtown that was on the passenger seat to show her.

"I was going to the library, but—Mehron—"

"Mehron went home. I can take you there." He smiled a little then. "Did you think she sent the text? I thought you'd figure it out by now, Whiz Kid."

Dulci felt breathless. Unable to form words. Happy. But how was he already feeling so perky, when she'd been so tired all day? "So you sent it."

"Yeah." He said it softly, his still-angular face softening as he looked at her. "So let's go then, huh? We've got stuff to talk about."

She placed her hands gingerly on the top of the driver's side door. "Jesse," she started.

"What, you want another one of these?" He reached out for her upper arm and pulled her in close. They kissed, his cheeks warming hers and her puffs of cloudy breath condensing around them. When he drew back, she stayed in place and said, "Yes. I do," and leaned further into the car to kiss him back.

When the hoots and cat-calls finally penetrated her consciousness, Dulci didn't care. She straightened, glanced around to see who was there. People she didn't know. She got into the El Camino, buckled in, and said, with a wave of her index finger, "To the library!" Jesse rolled his eyes, but then gave her a look of real affection, of new-forged hope.

Chapter 29

*   *   *

Neither Jesse nor Dulci was surprised when the town newspapers of 1777 now showed no violent agitation but the disappearance of one of the settlers, and the surrender of his land claim to an army installation. She could explain to Jesse the things she'd seen that hadn't been in order and which had confused her as well. Eventually, he told her the crafty lies that Taytere had been telling him for years, trying to motivate him to revenge. *Poor Angus,* Dulci thought. In all this, he was always the loser in any fight.

When the newspaper ran the story of the settler's disappearance, they'd included a short bio. Emigrating from Scotland at a young age, from wars and displacement in his home in the Highlands, he had landed here. He'd found a girl to marry but lost her in childbirth for their first child. She wondered if she asked Finn about his ancestor, if he would now say that he became a wandering wayfarer, and not a ghost. Maybe that was why he had forgotten the episode, so that he wouldn't have conflicting memories? Dulci's mind came up with many possibilities for the different effects and outcomes of their time travel, but it was all speculative.

Dulci never returned to that conversation with Mr.

McKenna, since he was transferred before Christmas to another school. She continued with her music club anyway, and wondered what he would say if she came across him in the supermarket one day. She wished she'd gotten to ask him about the other time travelers he knew. Perhaps one day, she would like to talk to them about her adventure.

Acknowledgements

I would like to say thank you to the many people who have advised, encouraged, promoted and championed my work and me throughout the writing and editing process. However, I don't have all day, or that good of a memory, so my apologies to those whom I forget.

Thank you to those on social media who have retweeted, commented, liked, and followed. These little measures of attention can mean a lot when you're struggling to get through a tough spot. Special thanks to Rooske de Joode and Sarah Brown, the two fastest-clicking fans!

Thank you to those who agreed to be beta readers and gave me the benefit of their input and impressions, within a short amount of turnaround time! The story changed quite a bit, so I hope you like how it turned out.

Thank you to Lauren Sweet, my first editor and someone who easily jumps into the adventure with a million ideas and delight in the editing process. That was definitely needed!

Thank you to the WDS solopreneurs, the Masterminds, the book club at Ward Stroud's, and all those unique, wonderful people of Portland who inspire and are inspired by life. Whenever you need a kick in the pants to readjust your frame, visit a Portland coffee shop, and you'll be reinvigorated.

And as the dedication says, thank you to my parents, who have grown in understanding as Dulci has.

A Note from the Author

Did you enjoy this book?

Please consider posting a review.

This helps self-published authors like me gain readers online and through word-of-mouth networks. You can post at any (or all!) of the following sites:

www.amazon.com
www.goodreads.com

Or spread the news through your own networks by recommending the book to your friends on:
www.facebook.com
www.twitter.com

Besides helping the book find its way to the hands of new readers, reviews can also be 'a light in dark places, when all other lights have gone out.'

My eternal thanks for your time, attention, and encouragement. *Until next time!*

About the Author

Margaret Pinard has spent her first few decades traveling the globe in search of adventures to incorporate into her writing, including living in the lands of the Celts, the cities of European fashion, and several dolce far niente Mediterranean cultures.

Her favorite genre is historical fiction, and she especially delights in fiction that makes you feel like you've been transported to a different time and place. Her first novel is *Memory's Hostage*. Her second, *Dulci's Legacy*, grew out of her first NaNoWriMo attempt in 2012. She resides in Portland, OR.